Dead Girls Can't Smile

Nichole Heydenburg

DEAD GIRLS CAN'T SMILE

Dead Girls Can't Smile

Copyright © 2024 by Nichole Heydenburg

Poisoned Ink Press LLC

All Rights Reserved. No part of this book may be used or reproduced in any manner whatsoever without written permission except in the case of brief quotations embodied in critical articles or reviews.

Contact Information: www.nicholeheydenburg.com

poisonedinkpress@gmail.com

Cover Design: Rocking Book Covers

Editors: BlackQuill Editing

Three Owls Editing

ISBN 978-1-961608-05-4 (eBook)

ISBN 978-1-961608-06-1 (paperback)

This book is a work of fiction. All characters, incidents, names, and places are utilized fictitiously or are the product of the author's imagination. Any similarity to real persons, living or dead, events, or businesses is completely coincidental.

Dedicated to Uncle John,
the one who introduced me to Stephen King books when I was only eleven.

Thanks for starting me on the road to loving all things dark and twisted and for reading every dark and twisted book I write.

Also by

Adult books:

The Long Shadow on the Stage- Book 1 in The Long Shadow Series

The Long Shadow of Memory- Book 2 in The Long Shadow Series

The Long Shadow of Death- Book 3 in The Long Shadow Series

DEAD GIRLS CAN'T SMILE

Young adult books (standalones):

The Quiet Girl- Revenge thriller

These Deadly Words- Supernatural thriller

Don't Look Inside- Psychological thriller

Dead Girls Can't Smile- Psychological thriller

Content warnings

kidnapping, child grooming, pedophilia, murder, swearing, underage drinking

Chapter 1: Lily

One year ago

Lily ran out of the woods, hopped onto her bike, and pedaled hard back toward her house. Tears flew down her cheeks, obscuring her vision. She sniffled and wiped her runny nose across her jacket sleeve. When she looked up, she spotted Spencer on her doorstep. He moved closer to her and stopped in front of her bike, blocking her from proceeding any further.

"Lily, I'm sorry about earlier, but you should go inside," he said in a gentle tone.

"I am," she replied, clearing her throat and trying to gather herself, although it was obvious she had been crying.

"Okay, goodnight," Spencer said, waving as he moved toward his house.

He went inside and shut the door. Lily waited a few more minutes to be sure, then she jumped back onto her bike and rode down the street, past her house and Spencer's, past all the neighbors she knew, until she was out of her neighborhood and on the main road.

Normally, the road outside of her neighborhood would be swarming with traffic and unsafe to ride her bike on. Her parents never let her leave the neighborhood by herself, but what they didn't know wouldn't hurt them.

It was after midnight. Her eyes strained through the darkness to see the white line for the bike lane. A small light on the front of her bike helped light her path a bit. She didn't have her reflective vest on, though. Her parents would be pissed if they knew how reckless she was being, but all she cared about was getting to his house. He would understand. He would comfort her like he always did and make her feel better.

Fresh tears rolled down her cheeks as she pedaled harder. If it wasn't for her stupid sister . . .

Lily turned her head to the right and left, checking that no cars were coming before she crossed the street to the neighborhood down the road from hers.

As she crossed, a car came speeding over the hill.

Lily hadn't seen it. The hill concealed the view. The car swerved, and Lily yanked her handlebars. She skidded toward the gravel on the road's edge. Her brakes screamed as she slammed down on them. The bike's front tire hit a rock. The jolt sent her forward. Lily flew from the bike, landing in a ditch several feet away.

A tall man stopped the vehicle and turned on the hazards, rushing over to her with long strides. "Oh God. Lily!" he screamed.

His feet slipped as he climbed down into the ditch. He regained his balance and bent over her, examining her frail body peppered with cuts and bruises from where the car had hit her. Her chest rose and fell, but she was holding on. Blood trickled from a wound on her head, and he pressed his hand to it. Blood dripped down his hand. He stared at it, open-mouthed, in horror.

"James . . ." she said, recognizing him.

His green eyes gazed down at her with regret.

James easily picked her up and cradled her to his chest. Lily groaned as he lifted her body, the pain excruciating. He brought her to his car and placed her in the backseat with care.

Her head was pounding, but she could still think somewhat logically, despite her injuries. "Where are we going? The hospital?" she asked.

James tossed her broken bike into his trunk and climbed into the driver's seat. "No, no one can know what happened. We have to go to my house now. I'll take care of you, Lily, I promise."

That's fine, Lily reasoned. James knew what to do. He would take good care of her, like he always promised he would.

"Okay," she whispered, her eyelids fluttering shut as she let the darkness overtake her.

Chapter 2: Rose

Present day

As Rose put her books in her backpack, she could have sworn someone was behind her. She whipped her head around to see the shadow of someone sneaking behind the corner. She quickly picked up her backpack and headed outside to meet Spencer, like she did every day.

While heading to the parking lot, she felt a presence looming behind her. She turned around, clutching her cell phone in her hand. Indistinct features were covered up by a baggy black hoodie, oversized sunglasses, and... *a mask*? Shading her eyes from the bright sunlight with her hand, she squinted to try to make out the person's features better. But as she squinted, they disappeared.

Rose turned around, glancing both ways down the sidewalk, but she didn't see anyone wearing a dark hoodie and sunglasses. She blinked rapidly a few times. They must have gone into one of the cars in the parking lot. She hadn't been able to tell which direction they went because the glaring sunlight made it impossible to see clearly.

She continued into the parking lot, where Spencer had been waiting for her, already in his car. Rose climbed into Spencer's car, threw her backpack into the backseat, and buckled her seatbelt.

"Drive!" she commanded.

With a bewildered expression, Spencer turned to her. "Wh—"

"GO!"

"What's wrong?" he asked.

Rose rolled her eyes. He knew better than to question her. After a slight hesitation, he obliged her wishes by backing out of the parking lot and heading down the road toward her house.

"Someone was following me," she whispered.

Spencer slammed on his brakes. "What? Who?" He glanced in the rearview mirror as if he was trying to see the person she was talking about.

Rose shook her head, and her wavy, red hair shrouded her face. "I don't know. They followed me from my locker out to the parking lot. It's so bright out I could barely tell it was a guy. He was wearing a dark hoodie and sunglasses with a mask on, so I couldn't see his face."

"Are you sure?" Spencer asked, driving again.

"Mmhmm. I think I know when someone's following me." Rose bit her lip and glanced behind them.

"Why would someone be following you?"

"I don't know!"

"Okay, geez. I'm only trying to help."

"Sorry. I'm freaked out. I didn't mean to take it out on you," Rose apologized.

"It's okay. Should we call the police? Or tell your parents? What do you want to do? Could it have something to do with Lily?"

Waves of ice-cold fear washed over her at the mention of her younger sister. It couldn't be connected to Lily. Whatever this was, it had nothing to do with her.

"No! This isn't about her. She's gone, Spencer. Just forget it."

Chapter 3: Lily

One year ago

When Lily woke up, James was shaking her. With a great effort, she kept her eyes open and sat up, but he pushed her back down into a horizontal position.

"Hey, it's okay. Lay down," James said. He smoothed the sweaty hair back from her forehead.

Lily surveyed the room, realizing she must be in his guest room. She had only been in there once before when he gave her a tour of his house the first time she came over. She was lying in a queen-sized bed with a quilt covering her body. The scent of cleaning products filled the room—disinfectant or bleach.

Across from the bed, several landscape paintings decorated the wall. A large oak dresser stood diagonally from the bed on the other side of the room, with an ornate gold mirror attached to it. Other than that, there were no furnishings—no TV, electronics, or books.

She couldn't see her reflection in the mirror from her position in the bed, but she could only imagine how disheveled she appeared. Her mind flashed back to what had happened, and she whimpered in pain as it all came back to her.

"James, I need to see a doctor." Lily held her hand to her head, touching the sore spot that must have hit the ground when she fell off her bike. Her head throbbed harder, as if the mere memory of what happened had intensified the pain.

"Shh, I'll take you to see one soon."

"Ugh, I think I'm going to be sick," she muttered, wrapping her arms around herself as her stomach roiled.

James whipped out a small trash can and handed it to her. Lily leaned forward, then heaved and vomited into the trash can, emptying the contents of her stomach until there was nothing left.

Isn't nausea a symptom of a concussion? She wracked her brain, trying to recall what she knew about head injuries, which wasn't much.

Crap. Her parents! They were going to be so worried about her.

"I need to get home," Lily said frantically, setting the trash can on the ground. "I can't stay here."

"Lily, it's okay. You'll be fine." James brushed his hand through her hair, soothing her. "I'll take care of you, my love."

"But my parents . . ."

James put a finger to her lips.

"How long was I unconscious?" she asked, speaking against his finger until he removed it.

James reached for her hand and held it as he answered. "About twelve hours. It's the next morning."

"Oh my God. My parents are going to kill me," Lily said with a groan. "I can't believe I've been gone all night. I've never done that before."

"Don't worry about that. You suffered a serious head injury last night. It's a miracle you made it through the night," James said in a nonchalant tone.

"James, this isn't funny! I can't stay here. It's—it's not right. My parents wouldn't like this. I need to get home," Lily said, becoming more agitated.

She tried again to get out of the bed, but James tucked her under the covers and kissed her forehead.

"Why would you want to go home? Don't you love me, Lily? I thought we were going to be together. I've sacrificed so much for you." James's tone became angrier, and his normally soft green eyes hardened. "Do you know how much trouble I would be in if anyone found out about us? I've risked my career, my life, everything—for you! Do you not care what could happen to me? Do you want me to go to jail? Is that all part of your grand plan, to frame me, to make me into the bad guy?" Spit flew from his mouth and sprinkled across her.

Lily wiped off the spit with disgust, but she hid her true emotions. "N-no, of course not. I want to go home," she whimpered.

James shook his head as his eyes softened again. "You can't go home, Lily. What would you tell your parents?"

"I c-could make up a story about falling off my bike and staying the night at a friend's house. I'll tell them I fell asleep and forgot to call to tell them I wouldn't be home."

"They won't believe you." He stared at her, his lip curling as he let go of her hand. "You're a mess. Besides, they know you don't have any friends. Except me, of course. But they don't know about me, do they?"

"No, I didn't tell them, I swear!"

Lily's heart beat faster as the reality of the situation sank in. James was refusing to let her go home. And he wouldn't take her to the hospital, even though she was hurt. He was going to let her leave, wasn't he?

She stifled a cry. She had to be strong. He couldn't keep her there forever. She could find a way out. She had to.

Chapter 4: Rose

Present day

Final exams flew by in a blur, and the last week of sophomore year ended. Rose slammed her locker and shoved the note into her backpack, checking both ways down the hallway to make sure no one noticed. Zipping her heavy backpack shut, she hoisted it onto her shoulders and proceeded to the double doors at the front of the school.

The school day was over, and Spencer would wait for her in the parking lot. Somehow, he always got out before her. When she met him at his car, he was already in the driver's seat, the air conditioning running at full blast.

Thank God. It had to be at least ninety degrees. Sweat dripped down her back as she slid into the passenger seat and tossed her backpack into the back seat.

"Hey, Rose," Spencer greeted with a grin.

"Hey, Spence. Do you want to get ice cream before you bring me home?"

"Is that even a question?"

Spencer backed out of the parking lot. Rose connected her phone to the car's Bluetooth and scrolled through a streaming service until she found Taylor Swift's new album.

Spencer fake grimaced as he recognized the song and shook his head.

"Whatever, you love it," Rose teased him as she caught him drumming his fingers on the steering wheel to the beat of the music.

Spencer rolled his eyes.

Ten minutes later, he parked in front of their favorite ice cream place, Hub City Scoops.

They strolled inside together, and an employee greeted them.

"Let me know if you want to taste any of the flavors!" A smile stretched across her heavily made-up face.

Spencer and Rose grinned at each other. They stepped forward to inspect the flavors for the week. Their flavors rotated constantly, and they loved trying the new ones every time. Spencer wasn't very adventurous, but he tried to be for her sake. Rose, on the other hand, would eat any food resembling ice cream.

After they had each tried three new flavors, Spencer picked cookie dough—so boring—and Rose chose a mixture of salted caramel and almond ice cream. Spencer held the door for her, and they left the store, licking their cones as they strolled down the sidewalk.

"How do you think you did on final exams?" Spencer asked.

"Ugh, you really want to talk about school right now? I've been studying so much that's the last thing I want to think about. It's officially summer, Spence!"

Spencer nudged her shoulder with his playfully. "Why wouldn't you want to think about school? You have the best study partner."

"Who?" Rose crinkled her nose in fake confusion.

"Okay, okay. Did you hear about the pool party tonight at Kasey McQueen's?"

"No, why? You weren't planning on going, were you?"

Spencer lifted one shoulder in an unsure gesture. "It might be fun."

"Do you have a crush on her or something?" Rose asked with a wicked grin.

Spencer snorted, and a chunk of ice cream flew off of his cone and onto the sidewalk. "Oops." He kicked it off to the side. "Nah, you know I don't like her like that. She's sweet, though."

With a final crunch, Rose finished the rest of her ice cream cone. "So, why would we go?"

"It's the first party of the summer! Sophomore year is over, and we're basically juniors now. I thought we could try something different this summer."

Rose sighed. "I thought I was supposed to be the adventurous one?"

Spencer snickered and licked ice cream off of his fingers. "I have to keep you guessing sometimes. Besides, I heard Mason will be there." He waggled his eyebrows.

A flush crept over her cheeks, and she ducked her head to hide her expression from Spencer. "Oh, well, in that case..."

"Uh-huh. That's what I thought. So, we can go?"

"Sure. I better get a new swimsuit before then."

"I'm sure whatever you already have is fine. Don't stress about it. It's only a party."

***

Later that night, Spencer picked her up for Kasey McQueen's party. Throughout the car ride, Rose became unbearably nervous, mostly because she hoped Mason would be there, but she didn't know how to act if he did show up.

When they arrived at Kasey's house, Spencer parked his car and glanced at her. "You okay?" He held out his hand.

"Yup."

She took his hand and clambered out of the car, only tottering slightly on her heels.

Spencer chuckled. "Can you even walk in those?" He gestured to her shoes.

"Of course I can." She squeezed his hand and pulled him along as she headed toward the front door.

When she almost tripped, she grabbed onto his shoulder to steady herself. Spencer burst out laughing.

"Are you going to make it?" He raised an eyebrow.

"*I'm fine*," she insisted.

Spencer was right, though. She was definitely not the type of girl who normally wore high heels or bikinis. Pursing her lips, she told herself it wasn't so Mason would finally notice her. She didn't want to be with the type of guy who only cared about her appearance. That was too much pressure. She wanted junior year to be different, and maybe that included having a hot boyfriend. Besides, she had several hot ex-boyfriends—and one extremely hot ex-girlfriend. None of those relationships had ended well. But Rose wasn't completely shallow. She cared about other things too, like getting into one of her top three choices for college and saving up for a car.

As they stepped up to the towering, two-story red brick house with a wraparound porch, Rose was in awe, despite the fact that she had been to Kasey's house several times before. It didn't make the house any less impressive.

Spencer rang the doorbell and turned to her with his hazel eyes sparkling. He opened his mouth as if he was about to say something, but the front door swung open, revealing a petite girl with a blonde bob and black, rectangular glasses.

"Hey! You guys made it!" Kasey squealed. She rushed forward and hugged each of them.

"Hey, Kasey," Rose said, smiling at her.

"Come in. Everyone's in the backyard." Kasey waved them inside and pointed to the back of the house.

Rose and Spencer followed Kasey down the hallway lined with photos of Kasey throughout her childhood. They went to the kitchen, where Kasey stopped in front of a long, white marble island. An overwhelming variety of drinks was on display—wine coolers, cheap beer, and a punch bowl full of a drink that resembled lemonade but probably wasn't.

"Help yourselves. I'll be out back." Kasey slipped out the patio door to the backyard and left them alone in the kitchen.

"Well, what do you think?" Spencer asked, staring at all the drinks.

"Hmm, maybe a wine cooler?" Rose inspected a slim can and picked it up.

Spencer grabbed a beer. "Okay, let's go. I'll only have one drink, so I can drive us home later."

"Good idea."

Spencer opened the patio door and gestured for her to go in front of him. "Ladies first."

Rose grinned. "Thanks."

Outside, Rose noticed there were about a dozen other students there from school, but no one else that she recognized besides Kasey.

Spencer headed toward Kasey, tugging Rose along with him. She followed nervously, wondering if it had been a bad idea to show up without knowing who would attend the party.

Kasey waved as they approached her. She was lying on one of the white-and-blue-striped lounge chairs in front of the pool. She patted the seat next to her. "Join me."

Rose and Spencer perched on the same chair, with Rose nearly sitting on Spencer's lap. She didn't want to leave his side. Her social anxiety kicked in at the thought of being left alone at the party. Or worse, being forced to make conversation with people she didn't know . . .

"So, what are your plans for the summer?" Kasey sipped from a glass of the lemonade-like substance that had been in the kitchen.

"Probably hanging out at the beach and making sure all of my college applications are finished, so I can send them in for early enrollment," Rose answered. She popped the tab on the wine cooler and took a tentative sip.

Kasey nodded. "Getting a head start on college applications is smart. I'll do the same. My parents are taking me on a cruise next week, but I should have time to work on my applications when we get back."

"Wow, where are you going?" Spencer asked, his hazel eyes wide.

Kasey smiled and leaned forward, clearly excited about her vacation. "The Bahamas. The cruise leaves from Florida next Wednesday . . ."

Rose didn't hear the rest of Kasey's sentence because the worst distraction had appeared. Kasey's words were drowned out by the appearance of an outrageously beautiful, tiny girl with shoulder-length, wavy blonde hair, pale skin, and blue eyes. *Holly Gray.*

"Did you know she was going to be here?" Rose whispered, clutching Kasey's arm, digging her nails into her bare skin.

Kasey yelped. "No, sorry, I didn't—"

"I have to go." Rose stood and set her drink on the concrete patio. She gestured to Spencer, who was still sitting on the lounge chair. "Spence, we need to leave. Now."

Spencer glanced at Holly. "Can't you avoid her so we can stay for a while? We just got here. We haven't even gone swimming yet."

Anxiety washed over her like the shock of a cold shower. She almost shivered, despite the sweltering South Carolina heat.

"I can't," she whispered. "I can't face her. Not after how it ended."

***

Sophomore year – August

Holly blinked her beautiful blue eyes at Rose. "Are you serious? Did you forget today is our six-month anniversary?"

Rose grimaced. She had forgotten—another way she was the worst girlfriend ever.

Holly crossed her arms over her chest. "Of course. Why am I surprised you forgot?"

"Did you . . . Did you have a date planned?" Rose asked, hoping the answer was no.

"Yes, but that doesn't matter now. Who am I supposed to take on this awesome date I've been planning all week?"

Rose moved closer to Holly, noticing the hurt in her normally hopeful eyes. She reached out for her, wanting to make her smile again, wanting to hold her in her arms.

But Holly uncrossed her arms and clenched her fists at her sides. "No. You don't get to touch me anymore. I gave you everything I had, and somehow, it wasn't good enough. I love you, Rose, more than I've ever loved anyone. And you destroyed my heart like it was nothing. You're going to rot in hell. I'll tell everyone what you did."

***

Present day

Kasey jumped up from her chair. "I swear I didn't invite her. I don't know why she showed up." She tilted her head to the side. "I can ask her to leave if you want?"

"Um, I don't know if that's a good idea. She'll probably get upset. You know she can be a drama queen. At least she came alone," Rose replied, hovering by the chairs and wringing her hands together as she debated what to do.

The sliding glass door slid open again, revealing a tall, muscular guy with slicked-back dark brown hair. He strode over to Holly and wrapped his arms around her, kissing her on the cheek.

"Oh my God." Rose sank back into the chair and wished she could disappear. "Are they together now?"

Spencer and Kasey openly stared at Holly and Reggie. Neither of them seemed to have an answer.

"I can't handle this," Rose whimpered.

"Two of your exes in one place? *And they're dating*? That's bad luck," Spencer said with a chuckle, shaking his head.

Holly and Reggie noticed them and headed their way.

"Shit," Rose muttered. "They're coming over here."

Spencer put his arm around her shoulder and pulled her close to him. "It's okay. I've got your back."

Chapter 5: Lily

One year ago

Turning over on the bed, Lily clutched her throbbing head. James had promised to bring her some painkillers hours ago, but he hadn't returned yet. Slowly, she sat up and took her time getting out of bed because her head ached painfully. She tiptoed over to the door and put her ear against it to see if she could hear anything. There was only silence. She turned the doorknob and tiptoed out of the room and down the hallway. Pausing, she peered down the hall, but she didn't see James.

Lily had been to his house many times, so she had the layout memorized. All those times she had lied and told her parents that she was hanging out with Rose and Spencer, riding her bike around the neighborhood, or staying after school for the photography club. She had quit the photography club months ago.

Instead, most days, James picked her up from the middle school. He had told any curious bystanders who witnessed her getting into his car that he was her uncle. Lily thought it was weird for him to claim to be her uncle, but she didn't question it. James was her friend, and he wouldn't hurt her. He cared about her more than anyone else did. Her parents didn't even know where she was half the time, and they definitely didn't notice when she was gone. Neither did Rose.

Lily crept down the familiar hall, her toes sinking into the soft, plush carpet. She stopped for a second to listen, but she still didn't hear a sound. Was that good or bad? She wondered what James was doing and where he was. At one point, she had thought she wanted to run away with him, but now she wasn't sure about that. He had refused to take her to the hospital or let her call her parents. He wasn't acting normal. Usually, he was so nice.

With a gasp, Lily spotted James coming around the corner. Lily ducked her head and turned to head back to the guest room, but he had already seen her.

James carefully gripped a wooden tray in his hands. The tray held a mug with steam curling up from it, toast, scrambled eggs, and two white pills.

"Lily! What are you doing out of bed? I was bringing you a late breakfast." James chuckled wryly. "Well, I suppose it's lunchtime now. I don't cook often. I couldn't find the frying pan or the spatula."

Lily stared at the tray, her stomach grumbling. She hadn't eaten since dinner with her family the night before.

"Are you hungry? Let's go back to your room and get you settled in." James gestured for her to follow him.

Lily obeyed him, but she didn't miss the fact that he had called it "her room," instead of the guest room.

When she was lying in the bed again, James set the tray on her lap.

"Dig in. Those painkillers should help your head. They're left over from when I had shoulder surgery a few years ago."

Lily glanced at the pills but didn't touch them.

"They're perfectly harmless." James leaned down to kiss her forehead.

Lily picked up the toast and took a bite, chewing abnormally slowly while he watched her eat. She cleared her scratchy throat. She hadn't drunk any water since the day before. "Thank you for cooking for me."

She smiled in what she hoped was a reassuring, trusting manner.

She needed to act like she was fine. Lily didn't feel safe with James anymore. Before, she had come over willingly. He had always given her a choice when they hung out. He hadn't forced her into anything. But now, he was being forceful and assertive. She didn't like the change in his personality or the fact that he hadn't taken her to the hospital when she had clearly suffered a serious head injury. Plus, when was he going to let her go home?

"How does it taste?" James leaned over the tray until his face was inches from hers. He picked up the two white pills. "Aren't you going to take these?"

Lily held out her hand, and he dropped the pills into her open palm. She didn't have any water, so she swallowed them forcefully with a few sips of the steaming tea.

"Thanks."

"You're welcome. If you're feeling better later, we can watch a movie."

"Okay, that would be fun. Can I pick?" Lily gazed up at him with hopeful eyes.

"Anything you want," he promised. "I'll leave you to finish your food in peace. I'll be back soon. If you need me, I'll be in my office."

Lily nodded and went back to eating the toast. James left the room. When he closed the door, she shoved the tray off of her lap.

Quietly, she stalked over to the lone window in the room. She couldn't bear another second in this house. Her parents and sister must be worried sick. She pushed aside the room-darkening curtains and gasped.

She let the curtains fall back into place. It would be impossible to escape through the window because it was shuttered. Thick, wooden boards were nailed across it.

Lily shivered, realizing she was no longer wearing her hoodie and jeans from the previous night. She was wearing sweatpants and a T-shirt. Had James taken off her clothes and put this new outfit on her? How had he known the right size to buy?

The more Lily thought about the situation, the more questions bombarded her mind. She didn't know how she would get out of here.

The question flew into her mind: what would Rose do?

Her older sister always knew what to do, the right choice to make, the smart move. Rose would probably try to convince James she was happy and everything was fine, lull him into complacency, and then strike when he wouldn't see it coming. She could do that. She just had to make sure he trusted her.

Lily had to live with him as his little pet until it was safe to escape.

Chapter 6: Rose

Present day

Holly stared her down, smiling widely and exposing her perfectly straight teeth as she stopped right in front of Rose. "Hi, Rose. I didn't know you would be here."

Rose chewed on her lip. "Well, I'm friends with Kasey. Why are you here?"

Holly laughed and flipped her wavy, blonde hair over her shoulder. "I don't need an invitation." Her eyes darted around the backyard and scanned the small crowd of people. "Although it isn't much of a party, is it?"

Reggie shook his head, agreeing with Holly. "Not our kind of party, anyway. Wanna leave? I heard there was a party at Jayce's tonight."

Holly snickered, her gaze lingering on Rose. "Not yet. I think we'll stick around a while and see if we can spice this place up." Holly leaned forward and wrapped her arms around Rose. "Great seeing you." She pulled away and stepped back, waving at Spencer and Kasey.

Reggie followed her.

Rose couldn't even muster a response. Plopping back down on a lounge chair, she snatched her drink from where she had set it on the patio. She chugged as much as she could and almost immediately felt it rush to her head. She didn't drink often. Rose and Spencer preferred playing video games and board games; they rarely went to parties.

"You okay?" Spencer asked.

Tears fell from her eyes as her mind drifted to her breakup with Holly. It wasn't entirely her fault. Holly had spread all those awful rumors about her afterward. But still . . . She knew Holly must hate her. So why had she approached her and hugged her? And why was she dating Reggie? As far as Rose knew, they couldn't stand each other.

***

Freshman year – January

"What the fuck, Rose?" Reggie mumbled, his dark eyes glinting with anger.

He shoved her into the wall, and she stumbled, grabbing the doorframe to stop herself from falling.

"You can't dump me! No one breaks up with me!"

Rose regained her balance and stepped backward, away from Reggie. She had chosen the school hallway in front of their lockers for a reason.

"I can, and I will. You're a jerk, Reggie. I can do so much better than you," Rose said.

"That's not what you were saying last week when we were—"

"Shut up. Sure, you're a good kisser, but that's about all you're good for. Maybe you can find a girl who doesn't care about anything else," Rose retorted with fire in her green eyes.

Reggie lunged for her. A tiny figure appeared. They jumped into the midst of the fray and slammed into Reggie's chest. Reggie screamed.

Rose kept her distance, unsure of the identity of the mysterious person.

"Leave her alone!" the stranger yelled.

Reggie lay crumpled in a pile on the linoleum flooring, rubbing his stomach.

A petite girl with shoulder-length, wavy blonde hair, pale skin, and the bluest eyes Rose had ever seen turned toward her and smiled. She couldn't have been taller than five foot two, but she somehow managed to be menacing.

The blonde stepped toward Rose and stuck out her hand. Her grin became wider. "Hi, I'm Holly. Holly Gray."

***

Present day

"I think so, but that was weird, right?" Rose asked, eyeing her friends for confirmation.

"Yup, definitely weird," Kasey agreed. She straightened out the straps of her bikini and smiled softly. "Did you two bring swimsuits? Wanna swim?"

"Um, sure. Do you know if Mason is coming?" Rose asked.

Kasey smirked. "So you can make Holly jealous?"

"What? No! I'm over her. I just . . . I—" Rose stuttered.

"She likes Mason," Spencer said with an eye roll. "You have terrible taste, for the record."

Rose's gaze wandered to Holly and Reggie at the other end of the yard. Reggie stood in the shallow end of the pool splashing Holly, who was sitting on the edge of the pool and dangling her tanned legs in the water. Holly squealed as Reggie soaked her.

"Stop! Don't ruin my hair," Holly chastised him.

"How did you put up with her? She acts like such a princess." Spencer grimaced and sipped his beer.

Rose shrugged. "She was different with me. Not the same as she acts in public. Besides, she's—"

"Gorgeous? Has a killer body? Eyes you could get lost in? And perfect hair?" Kasey blurted out.

"Well, yes, that too," Rose replied, her face flushing.

"Are we going to swim or spend all day talking about your past relationships? This summer is supposed to be different. Focus on our future and all that," Spencer said.

"You're right." Rose slipped her thin, gauzy white dress over her head and tossed it onto the chair, revealing a teal bikini and her flat stomach.

Spencer soon followed suit, taking off his T-shirt. He was already wearing his swim trunks.

"Let's go!" Kasey called, racing them to the pool.

Rose and Spencer took off after her, giggling as they all jumped into the pool. Spencer did a cannonball that soaked Holly; she and Reggie left soon afterward.

They swam for a while, and Rose forgot about Mason. Instead, she enjoyed a summer afternoon with her friends.

***

The next day, Rose sprawled out on a towel on the beach, sunglasses perched on her nose and an immense amount of sunscreen covering her pale skin. Spencer lay next to her reading a comic book while she checked all her social media accounts.

Spencer set his comic on his towel, partially covering it so it didn't get covered in sand. "What are you doing?"

Rose finished tagging the local beach—Leopold Beach—on a picture of the sunlight reflecting off of the water with a sliver of sand at the bottom. "Nothing." She tossed her phone into her tote bag and stretched her arms out. "Wanna go swim for a bit?"

"Sure."

Rose approached the gentle waves, slowly inching into the cool water. Spencer chased her, grabbed her around the waist, lifted her into his arms, and threatened to throw her in.

Screaming, Rose hit him on the chest until he put her down. "You're such a jerk sometimes."

"You know you love me." He beamed at her before taking off deeper into the water.

Soon, they were tired and couldn't handle much more of the heat. Summer days in South Carolina could be brutal.

"Ready to head out?" Spencer asked as they walked back to the spot where they had left their towels and belongings on the beach.

"Yeah, let me pack up my stuff first." Rose rolled up her towel and shoved it into her bag. She rearranged her hastily thrown in belongings to make it all fit.

A handwritten note fluttered out of her bag and onto the sand.

"What is that?" Spencer pointed to the note and leaned down to pick it up.

Rose darted for it before he could grab it, remembering the note she received yesterday. In her haste to get home that day, she had forgotten about the note, but this was the second one she had received. Panic flitted throughout her body as her fingers wrapped around the note. *Who is leaving them? Is someone following me?*

She took in the sights of the beach, not quite sure what she was looking for. Rose scanned the adults and kids laying on towels and picnic blankets, swimming in the lake, building sandcastles, and applying sunscreen. No one familiar. Nothing out of place.

"Rose? What is it?" Spencer leaned toward her, placing a gentle hand on her shoulder.

Rose's gaze dropped to the note clutched in her hand, grains of sand now dusting it. "Um, I think . . . I think someone is stalking me."

Chapter 7: Lily

Ten months ago

"Darling, do you want spaghetti for dinner?" James called from the kitchen.

Two months had passed since Lily had started keeping track of time. James had the summer off, so he had spent every waking second with her. July and August had crawled by, and it was September now. Lily would have given anything to be back at school, even without any friends, to get out of this house where she was a prisoner.

James was back at work full-time. She relished the moments during the day when he was gone, when she had time to herself to think about how to escape.

Every day, she wondered if her parents and Rose had given up on finding her or if they were still searching. Did they have a search party? Did the police have any leads? No one knew about James, so she didn't know what conclusion they would reach. Lily speculated about what they thought had happened . . . if they assumed she had been kidnapped and killed. Or maybe that she ran away from home. She couldn't bring any of these questions up to James, so she lived out the lie the best she could, waiting for an opportunity to break out.

"Sure, spaghetti sounds good!" she responded, shutting the paperback book she had been reading and setting it on the coffee table.

If James was in a good mood, then he let her out of the bedroom. Today was one of those days, so she had sprawled out on the couch in the living room, enjoying her tiny piece of freedom while it lasted. Lily had adjusted to living with him. The last few days had been quiet, peaceful. It was only a matter of time before she accidentally pissed him off, though. It was always unintentional, but it didn't matter. She hadn't seen this side of him until they had moved in together—or rather, until he had kidnapped her. James was scary when he was angry, and he didn't calm down easily. Once he was upset, sometimes it took a full day for him to return to normal.

Lily was still confused about what he expected from her and whether he thought they could continue like this for the rest of their lives. After two months, she was beginning to think there was something wrong with him. She felt stupid for not noticing it sooner. Before, she had been so happy that James paid attention to her. He called her pretty and brought her nice gifts all the time. James was her first real boyfriend. She had thought she was in love with him. Now she wasn't sure she knew anything.

Lily took a seat at the kitchen table. James set a steaming plate of spaghetti and meatballs topped with parmesan in front of her. He went to the counter and came back with a basket of Texas toast and a bowl of green beans.

"Thank you, James. This looks delicious." Lily picked up her fork and twirled the spaghetti around it.

James grabbed her wrist, halting her movements.

Her green eyes darted to his hand on her wrist. She dropped the fork. "What's wrong?" she asked, her voice already beginning to waver.

"Do you have to be so formal with me?" He stroked her wrist and let go. "We can finally be together, but I don't think you appreciate me anymore. Have you become bored with me? Is there someone else?" His eyes narrowed at her menacingly.

Lily fidgeted with her Texas toast, tearing it into pieces and scattering them across her plate but not eating. "No. How could there be anyone else when I've been trapped in here for two months?"

Uh oh. She regretted her word choice when rage clouded James's face.

His nostrils flared. "*That's it!* I cooked this nice dinner for you, and you don't care? Do you even want to be with me? Why did you say you're trapped here when all you talked about for months was escaping your home? I did you a favor!" he screamed.

He stood and yanked her out of her chair, pushing her toward the hall. "Go to your room."

"But . . . but what about dinner?" Lily asked, whimpering as her socked feet slid on the linoleum floor. She reached out a hand to steady herself against the table so she didn't fall.

James's face turned into an impassive mask. "You can eat after you've had time to think about your actions. You can eat tomorrow morning if your behavior changes."

Lily had no intention of listening to him. She had been stuck in the house for two months, so she had thought about her options to escape. There was the front door—the most obvious option—but it would be hard to reach it without James catching her. It was at the other end of the hallway, past the kitchen and living room. Whenever he left the house, which was rare aside from when he went to work, he locked her in the guest room.

Besides that, there was a garage door where he stored his car and motorcycle. There were also various windows in the main living space, but she hadn't been able to check if those were boarded up too. Even if they weren't, she would probably have to punch out or remove the screen to climb out of a window. The home was old, and the windows were tiny. She was small for a twelve-year-old, but she didn't know if she could fit through a window.

Since she was in the kitchen, she decided to make a run for the front door. It was her best option. Lily darted for the front of the house, sliding across the hallway in her socks. *Crap.* She would have probably had a better chance if she was barefoot, or better yet, wearing shoes. The door was mere feet away. Lily heard James's chair clatter to the ground, but she didn't want to turn around.

There were two deadbolts on the door. Did she have enough time to unlatch both? Her fingers reached out to touch the first one as a snarl erupted from much too close behind her. James's fingers encircled her wrist, dragging her away from the door.

"Ow! You're hurting me," Lily protested.

"Why are you trying to leave, Lily? I've given you everything you ever wanted," James said. His face was red, and he was breathing loudly.

Lily didn't respond.

"Maybe twenty-four hours without food will make you appreciate how good your life is," he said in a cold tone.

Resigned, Lily obeyed his wishes and went into the guest room. She couldn't bear to think about it as her bedroom, although it technically was. She didn't plan on staying here forever. The lock clicked, and she knew James had locked her in the room for the night. The lock was on the outside of the door, so there was no way out.

At least the tiny en-suite bathroom meant she could use the restroom if she needed to. Being trapped in the room without a bathroom would be worse. In this situation, she had to appreciate the small things.

Unfortunately for Lily, the bathroom didn't have a window. At this point, she had gone over every possible means of escape. She wasn't giving up yet, though. She would have to wait and try again.

Sinking down onto the bed, Lily stared around the room for the millionth time. She didn't have a TV or books or any form of entertainment in here, really. Those items were rewards if she did exactly as James wished.

Her best chance of escape was waiting until James was gone. Otherwise, she didn't think she could make it far enough away before he noticed. When he was home, he was constantly checking on her and watching her. It was unnerving. He wanted to spend every waking moment with her. Or he was extremely paranoid about her leaving.

Next time James left the house, she had two options. Either she could convince him to let her go with him, or she could convince him to leave her home alone—but not locked in the guest room. Neither option was great, but if she went out with him in public, there could be multiple opportunities for her to get away from him, find a phone to call the police, or ask someone for help.

With nothing better to do, Lily pulled the quilt over her body and shivered uncontrollably. Summer was ending, and fall was approaching. The room grew chillier each day. She wanted to ask James for an extra blanket or for him to turn up the heat, but she would be pushing her luck if she asked him for a favor.

Lily fell asleep dreaming about her parents and Rose finding her and rescuing her. If she reunited with her family—that was all she wanted—she would never ask for anything again.

Chapter 8: Rose

Present day

Back at home, Rose sat on her full-sized bed, still holding the note in her hand. She had dug through her backpack to find the first note she discovered in her locker yesterday.

"Are you going to show them to me?" Spencer popped the tab on a can of soda and joined her on the bed.

"Yes, but I don't know what they say." Rose met his eyes carefully. "The first one was in my locker yesterday."

Spencer raised an eyebrow. "Why didn't you tell me sooner?"

"I—I don't know," she stuttered. "I guess I forgot."

"Rose, I'm your best friend. If you can't talk to me about receiving weird notes and having a stalker, then who else do you have?"

Sighing, Rose unfurled the crumpled note in her hand. "You're right. I really did forget about it, though."

She straightened out the note on her bed as best she could and read the slanted handwriting:

Rose,
I admire your strength and beauty. You aren't like the other girls at school. You're so much better than them.
Your Secret Admirer

"Hmm, romantic or creepy?" Spencer mused, staring at the note.

"A secret admirer?" Rose crinkled her nose. "That's not what I was expecting."

Spencer started laughing. "Would you rather have an actual stalker?"

"Well, no, but leaving handwritten notes for someone is so old-fashioned. Why wouldn't they follow me on social media or ask for my phone number to text me?"

Spencer's eyes drifted to the ceiling like he was deep in thought. "Maybe they do follow you on social media. It must be someone who knows you if they knew which locker was yours. They must go to our school."

"Good point." Rose unfolded the second note and laid it out next to the first one.

"Wait, the handwriting is different in this one," Spencer said as soon as she set it down. He picked both notes up to compare them. "I don't think they were written by the same person."

"I think you're right. So, I have two secret admirers?" Her eyes widened.

"Uh, not quite. Read the second note."

My dearest Rose,
You thought you would get away with it, but I know your secret about the night your sister went missing. I'm going to make sure you pay for what you did, you little liar.
The Midnight Flower

Chapter 9: Lily

Nine months ago

The front door slammed. Moments later, he came into the guest room, whistling.

Lily sat on the bed, unmoving. James joined her on the bed and took her hands in his.

"What? No hello kiss?" he teased.

Lily frowned. "No."

"Why aren't you happy to see me? What's wrong, my perfect flower?" James asked, squeezing her hand.

"Everything!" she screamed, throwing his hands from hers. She jumped up from the bed, kicking him hard in the chest, and startling him so much that he fell back.

Lily darted for the bedroom door, swinging it open and not bothering to grab her shoes. She raced down the hallway and toward the front door, her bare feet barely touching the faux-hardwood floors. She heard a startled noise from him and kept going. Too late to stop now.

She was so close. She reached for the door, fumbling to unlock the two deadbolts. The second one clicked as it unlocked, and she turned the doorknob.

The scent of crisp fall air and burning leaves from a house nearby hit her as soon as she was outside. Lily had never thought she would miss those smells, but she had missed everything about the outside world.

Her feet pounded down the driveway as she continued, glancing back to see James coming out the front door, mere feet behind her.

With a yelp, Lily kept going, pushing herself further, her legs beginning to ache as she made it to the street. She realized with an uncomfortable jolt that she had let herself become lazy over the past three months. She should have spent her free time building up endurance, preparing herself for an escape. Any second now, he would catch up to her and bring her back to his lair. And it would be her own fault.

She cried out for help, swinging her arms wildly as she ran down the street.

"Lily!" he yelled from behind her.

She heard his footsteps approaching. Too close. She turned around and screamed. James clapped his hand down over her mouth. He wrapped his arms around her midsection, carrying her kicking and screaming back into the house.

When they were inside, he locked the door again and brought her into the guest bedroom.

Before he left, he gave her a warning that chilled her to the bone. "If you ever pull a stunt like that again, I'll kill you. I've given you two chances now. You think you're special? You aren't the first girl I've let live with me, and you might not be the last. You have a lovely smile, but there will always be other girls who are even more lovely." He paused, malice burning in his eyes. "And you can easily be replaced. Dead girls can't smile, Lily. Remember that." He shut the door, and she heard the lock outside the door click.

Lily was trapped. During the past three months, she had avoided thinking about her fate, but the direness of the situation was sinking in after his recent admission. This whole time, she had tried to convince herself she loved James and he loved her, but what if that wasn't true? What did he mean by 'other girls?'

Trembling, she sat on the edge of the bed, debating the best path forward. More than ever, she wanted to survive. She wanted to live. Was she willing to give up her freedom for a life that might not be worth living?

Chapter 10: Rose

Present day

Rose couldn't bear to think about that terrible night, but now it was at the forefront of her mind. She and Spencer were the only ones who knew what happened . . . besides one other person. But they wouldn't have told. They cared about Rose, or at least they used to.

"You didn't tell anyone, did you?" Rose asked, worry lacing her tone as she bit her lip.

"No, of course not!" Spencer gave her a side-eye. "Did you?"

"No!" she lied.

"Okay, then let's not accuse each other because we're on the same side. We're the only ones who know. They must be talking about something else. Do you have any secrets you haven't told me?" Spencer asked with a wry smile.

"No, that's it, and it's bad enough. I don't want to talk about it," Rose huffed.

Rose took the note from Spencer, got off of her bed, and went to her desk. She ignored the framed picture of her sister, her wavy, red hair shining like copper in the sunlight, her mouth open, exposing her slightly crooked teeth as she laughed hysterically. Rose opened the bottom drawer of the desk and put the notes underneath a stack of notebooks, then locked the drawer with a key hidden in her nightstand.

"There, now we're the only ones who know where the notes are. Let's keep this between us, okay? At least until we can figure out what's going on or who's leaving these notes. If they leave another one, there might be a clue that can help us," Rose suggested, leaning against her desk.

"Okay, if that's what you want," Spencer answered, his voice wavering uncertainly.

Rose narrowed her green eyes. "What? You don't think we should tell someone, do you?"

Spencer shrugged his shoulders. "Besides your parents, who would we tell?"

"Exactly. We can't trust anyone, especially not if it involves . . . well, you know."

"You're probably right. We won't get anyone else involved unless the situation becomes dangerous," Spencer agreed.

"*Dangerous*? Do you think they'll try to hurt us? All they've done is leave two notes." Rose's chest became tight and full of fear about what someone would do to them if they knew the truth. After all, they hadn't just lied to her parents—they had lied to the police too.

"Well, the notes are both directly addressed to you . . ." Spencer started.

"Why is that? Wouldn't they be after both of us if they knew our secret? Why didn't you get a note?"

"I don't know, Rose. No matter what, we're in this together. I'll help you get to the bottom of this," Spencer promised.

***

After Spencer left, Rose's parents made lasagna for dinner. The scent of ground beef cooking wafted up to Rose's bedroom. Her stomach grumbled as she imagined a steaming plate full of her mom's homemade lasagna. It had been one of Lily's favorite meals too.

Rose distracted herself from thinking about Lily by starting a new game of *Zombies Attack*. Slashing through decaying zombie flesh with an ax was a great stress reliever.

Shortly after, her mom called her downstairs to join them. "Rose! Dinner's ready," her mom yelled from the bottom of the staircase.

"Coming!" Rose yelled back, pressing pause on her controller.

She bounded down the stairs and greeted her parents. Rose's mom, Celia, worked as a middle school teacher, so she was home more often than usual during the summer. In the past, it didn't bother Rose, but after Lily went missing, her mom's hovering and overprotectiveness could be a bit much.

"I haven't seen you much the last few days. Were you with Spencer?" her mom asked with a nervous edge to her voice.

"Yeah, we went to the beach today," Rose replied nonchalantly, grabbing a plate from the cupboard.

"Which one?" her dad interjected. "I was watching the news earlier. They said the lake has unusually high levels of bacteria, so it isn't safe to swim in the water. Were you swimming?"

"Charlie, I'm sure she's fine. Rose is old enough to know better," her mom defended her. She cut off a piece of the gigantic lasagna, placed it on Rose's plate, and handed it to her.

Rose avoided answering their questions, especially since she had gone swimming. It wasn't like she had watched the news and knew about the warning.

"Did you make garlic bread too?" Rose asked.

Her mom handed her a piece of garlic bread and smiled. "Of course, extra cheese for you."

Her dad grimaced and mumbled a complaint about putting cheese on everything.

Her mom handed him a plain slice of garlic bread. "I heard you grumbling, so I made some *without cheese* specially for you."

"More for me." Rose took the plate from her mom and sat at the kitchen table.

"Spencer didn't want to stay for dinner?" her mom inquired with a raised eyebrow.

Spencer frequently ate meals at their house. In fact, he rarely left.

"No, his mom wanted him home to spend some time together." Rose reached for the parmesan on the table and sprinkled it over all of her food. She stabbed the lasagna with her fork and took a bite.

"What are your plans for the summer?" her dad asked.

"College applications, hanging out with Spencer, and relaxing before school starts again." Rose tore off a piece of cheesy garlic bread and dunked it into marinara sauce. "Mmm, thanks for cooking, Mom."

"You're welcome, Rose. Do you have plans for tomorrow? Can we go see a movie or go shopping? Girls' day out?" her mom asked as she finally joined Rose and her dad at the table.

"Sure, that sounds fun. We could see the new *Saw* movie?"

Her mom's blue eyes sparkled with mischief. "Oh, yeah! Let's go see that. I forgot a new one was coming out this month."

"What else is going on?" her dad asked.

"What do you mean?" Rose hurriedly swallowed the bite of garlic bread she had shoved into her mouth.

"Oh, I don't know. I thought I heard you and Spencer whispering about something or other in your bedroom earlier. Are you two okay?" Her dad peered at her closely, wrinkling his forehead with concern.

"Yup, fine. We're both fine," Rose said, her eyes dropping to her plate and willing herself to believe it was true.

So she had received two mysterious notes from strangers. That didn't mean anyone was going to hurt her or that she was in danger. Rose was perfectly safe as long as her secret didn't get out. Although Rose was starting to wonder if the person she had once trusted with all her secrets had betrayed her.

The only other person who knew the truth was Holly.

Chapter 11: Lily

Nine months ago

James hadn't let her out of the guest room in at least twenty-four hours. Through the curtains in her bedroom, Lily had seen the sun set and rise again the next morning. She wondered if he would ever let her out. He had sounded so angry when he yelled at her yesterday. What if he never came into the room again and she died in here alone?

Lily lay in the bed like she usually did when James locked her in the guest bedroom. She had become accustomed to lying in silence and going an entire day—sometimes longer—without talking to another living soul or being able to eat. James claimed she was perfect, so she didn't understand why he would deprive her of food. If she lost much more weight, she would wither away to nothing.

The doorknob turned. This time, Lily didn't bother getting out of bed or greeting him. She was sick of his games.

"Hello, Lily," James said with a smile, holding a tray filled with food toward her.

She didn't respond.

A frown replaced his smile. "I have to leave for work in ten minutes. I brought you breakfast."

"Great. Thanks," Lily said in an apathetic tone. She took the tray from his hands and set it on her lap, picking up an apple.

James was fuming now. His face turned bright red, and Lily pictured smoke coming out of his ears, like in a cartoon.

"You ungrateful slut! You don't appreciate all that I do for you. I work my ass off every day to provide all this for you." He gestured wildly around the room. "I thought your attitude would improve, but clearly, it hasn't."

James yanked the tray out of her hands, spilling hot tea across Lily's lap.

"Watch out!" she screeched, jumping back.

"Look at the mess you made. You stupid girl. Clean it up." With the tray of food in his hands, James left the room, glancing back as he moved down the hall. "I was going to let you out of your room today, but don't think about it now. If you're good when I get home, you can eat dinner tonight."

Lily sprang forward, darting around the spilled tea that had dripped down the quilt. She went into the hall toward him. "No! James, please, I'm so hungry. Can I at least have the fruit?" She hungrily eyed the bowl of mixed fruits on the tray.

James laughed and stared down at her. "I don't think so."

"Wait! Please, can I have something to eat?" Lily kneeled on the faux-hardwood floor and clasped her hands together, begging James to take pity on her.

"You're pathetic. I can't look at you." James straightened his tie and pointed to the guest room. "Get back in there. You aren't leaving today."

Lily whimpered. "But, James, I'll starve. I'm so weak already. I don't know how much longer I can go without eating."

"You should have thought about that before you disobeyed me. Do I really ask that much of you? I'm not impossible to please. You just need to learn your lesson. Now get in there. If I'm late to work because of you, there will be hell to pay."

Lily believed him. She didn't want to take the chance of pissing him off so much that he hurt her, so she retreated into the guest room and climbed into bed. James shut the door, and she heard the lock click.

A heavy sense of doom settled over her. She clutched one of the pillows in between her hands and silently screamed into it. Her fate was sealed.

Chapter 12: Rose

Present day

Thunder rumbled in the distance, and a crack of lightning lit up her previously darkened room. Rose fumbled for her phone and turned on the flashlight. Crawling out of bed, she made her way to her window, where her thin, lacy curtains swayed from the wind. She peered out the window to see the rain pelting against the side of the house, but the eeriest part of the scene was the mysterious figure in a black hoodie and mask taking off down the street.

Rose stuck her head out the window to identify the mysterious person, but the rain soaked her almost immediately. After shutting the window, she towel-dried her hair and climbed back into her bed. The mysterious person running down the street had come from the direction of her house, but who was it? The hooded figure who had been following her the past few days? The same person who kept leaving her notes?

Rose made sure her toes weren't poking out from underneath her blanket and wrapped the covers around her body, cocooning her body in warmth to convince herself she was safe. After twenty minutes of tossing and turning and obsessing over the potential stalker, she decided to wake up her parents.

She knocked on their bedroom door. When she didn't receive an answer, she said, "Mom? Dad? Someone was outside the house."

That got a quick response. The door flung open, making her stumble off balance and grapple for the doorframe to steady herself. Her dad stood in the doorway wearing a T-shirt and sweatpants. He reached out to touch her shoulder gently.

"What did you say? Someone's outside?" He peered down at her with a crease forming on his forehead.

She nodded. "The thunder woke me up. I fell asleep with my window open because it was hot. I went over to the window to close it and saw someone outside."

Rose felt like she had when she was a little kid, waking up her parents in the middle of the night when she had a scary nightmare. But she didn't know what else to do. If she couldn't rely on her parents, who else could she go to for help? That was their responsibility—to keep her safe.

"Okay," her dad said, turning to face the king-sized bed on the far side of the room. "It's okay, Celia. Go back to sleep. I'll deal with it." Her dad beckoned for Rose to move, and he closed the bedroom door.

Rose noticed a small handgun in his right hand. It had been tucked behind his back before that.

"Why do you have that?" she asked, pointing at the gun.

"I'm not going to investigate without a weapon. You should know better than that, Rose. All those days we spent at the shooting range weren't for nothing, right?" He smirked as if he was trying to lighten the terrifying situation. "Go back to sleep and lock your bedroom door. I'll deal with this," her dad promised.

***

All too soon, the sunlight peeked through the curtains and invaded Rose's bedroom. Groaning, she turned over and buried her face into her pillow to block out the light. Her phone buzzed from wherever she had left it last night, and she finally climbed out of bed, scrambling to find it. There weren't many people who would call her on a Sunday morning in the summer.

Rose found her phone on her desk, next to her bedroom door. She must have dropped it there last night when she came back to her room. She picked it up to see who was calling her. The incessant buzzing continued, and she spotted Spencer's name.

"Hello?" she answered.

"Geez, it's about time! I've been texting and calling you all morning," Spencer replied in an agitated tone.

"Sorry, I just woke up." Rose yawned and covered her mouth with her hand. "I didn't get much sleep."

"Evidently."

"Why did you call?"

"What are we doing today?" Spencer asked.

"Oh, right. I forgot to tell you I have plans with my mom today. She wants us to have a 'girls' day." Rose sighed as she remembered.

"Oh, okay. Can we hang out tomorrow, then?"

"Sure."

Silence ensued while Rose thought about the hooded figure whom she had spotted leaving her house last night.

"Spence?"

"Yeah?"

"Someone was at my house last night. I think it was—"

"WHAT?" Spencer yelled so loudly that she winced and held the phone away from her ear.

"I woke up my dad because I was scared. He told me to go back to my room, and he—"

"What did your dad do? What happened? Did he catch whoever it was?" Spencer blurted out question after question.

"Uh . . . I'm not sure. I must have fallen asleep. I should probably go make sure he's okay."

"Rose, please be careful. If someone is stalking you, maybe you should tell your dad about the notes. Do you think—"

"No, I can't tell him, because then I'll have to tell him about our secret, and I won't do that. My parents can't find out," Rose said fervently.

"Okay. Maybe you shouldn't leave the house today. Stay home and watch a movie with your mom there?" Spencer suggested.

"I'll be fine. They won't try anything if I'm with my mom. Talk to you later."

"Call me if you need me. Bye, Rose."

Rose ended the call and tossed her phone onto her bed, where she sat down and put her head in her hands. She sat still for a moment before she scouted out her closet for a suitable outfit for a day out with her mom. After she was ready, she went downstairs to find her parents. She wanted to ask her dad what had happened last night, and hopefully, that would be the end of it.

Her dad sat on the tan leather couch, sipping orange juice and watching the news. He put the TV on mute and patted the seat next to him on the couch. Tentatively, Rose joined him.

"Good morning. Did you sleep okay?" he asked.

"Morning, Dad. I got some sleep. What happened last night? Did you see anyone?"

Her dad frowned, setting his glass of orange juice on the coffee table in front of the couch. "No. It was raining pretty hard, so I grabbed the umbrella. I took off down the street and checked the side streets nearby too, but I didn't see anyone outside. I called the police, but they took forever to show up. They didn't find any evidence of someone lurking around the house." He paused before he continued. "Are you sure you saw someone outside last night? You were tired. If the storm woke you up and scared you, it wouldn't be strange if you imagined something."

"I didn't imagine it, Dad. Someone was there, I swear!" Rose protested.

"Okay, okay. I believe you. I think you need to rest today. Don't go to that movie. Your mom went grocery shopping, but she should be back soon. Tell her you want to stay here and hang out."

"No, I'm fine. I'll go to bed early tonight. Mom will be disappointed if I cancel our plans. I want to hang out with her. I think getting out of the house and seeing a movie will distract me for a while," Rose pleaded.

"Well, okay. Can't argue with that. You'll tell me if you see anything else suspicious, won't you?"

"Of course."

But Rose knew involving her dad hadn't been her smartest idea. He already had one missing daughter—he didn't need to worry about her too. A stalker, creepy notes, and feeling unsafe in her own home... How was this summer already going so badly?

Chapter 13: Lily

Seven months ago

James woke her up with a mischievous grin and handed her a box wrapped with shiny red paper and a sparkly silver bow on top. Lily stared at the box, wondering what was inside. Over the months, she had kept track of time with a spare piece of paper she found one day in the living room. She kept it hidden underneath her mattress. But it was still difficult to accept that it was already Christmas.

Her heart ached as she remembered all the past Christmases spent with her family. Her mom always cooked barbeque meatballs in the Crock-Pot, and they would spend most of the day watching the old Christmas movies from the '70s, like *Santa Claus is Comin' to Town* and *The Year Without a Santa Claus.* Then Lily and Rose would sip hot chocolate with dozens of tiny marshmallows and open their gifts as their parents watched with eager anticipation. Spencer and his mom always came over too, which had become a part of their family traditions after Spencer's dad left.

"Are you going to open it?" James asked. The excited grin had vanished from his face. His brow furrowed, and she could tell the hard, angry glint was going to take over his face soon if she didn't rectify the situation.

"Ye-yes. Thank you. Merry Christmas!" she said with fake enthusiasm, tearing the red paper off of the box and ripping the tape to open the gift. She had learned that it was easier to pretend to be happy around him.

"Do you like it?" James sat next to her on the bed and put his arm around her, holding her close to him.

Lily blinked at the silky item in the box. She picked it up carefully and held it out with two fingers, like it was a bug or something equally gross, examining it. "A fancy bra?"

"Only the best lingerie for you, my perfect flower." James kissed her on top of her head. "You can model it for me later." He winked and headed toward the door. "I'll leave you to get dressed and ready for the day."

Lily set the lingerie back in the box and sat up straighter. "Get ready? Are we going somewhere?"

"Only if you're good," he threatened.

"Where are we going?"

Hope bloomed inside of her. She didn't want to seem too eager, but this was what she had been waiting for—the perfect chance to escape. This was it.

"It's a surprise." He blew her a kiss and left the room.

Lily scrambled out of bed, hurrying to put on a pair of pants and a sweater. At least James had the decency to buy her warmer clothes for the winter, although she knew he preferred it when she wore tank tops and shorts—clothes that exposed her skin as much as possible.

All she had to do was pretend to be excited that he was taking her on a date. That shouldn't be too difficult, considering she *was* excited—excited to get away from him.

Chapter 14: Rose

Present day

Rose and Spencer sat across from each other in a red vinyl booth. She snatched another slice of pizza from the tray in the center of the table. Pepperoni, sausage, and black olives was their go-to order at Pi Squared, a local pizza place known for their Detroit style, deep-dish pizza.

"Did you play the new update of *Zombies Attack*?" Spencer asked.

Rose nodded with her mouth full of pizza.

"Do you want to hang out and play it after we eat?"

Rose swallowed the bite of pizza and took a sip of soda to wash it down. "Heck yeah! We've been waiting for this update forever. I've gotta warn you, though. Since I haven't been able to sleep, I've been playing a lot lately."

"So, what? You think you're better than me at killing zombies?" A devious grin spread across Spencer's face.

"Yeah, right. I *know* I'm better than you."

"Game on, babe. It's on."

The waitress brought over the check and placed it between them on the table. Spencer grabbed it before Rose had pulled out her wallet.

"I'll pay for it," Spencer said.

"Oh, well, thanks." Rose blushed.

The waitress took the credit card with a quiet, "Thank you."

Rose and Spencer each finished another slice of pizza, leaving half of the pizza remaining.

"I guess we need a box," Spencer told the waitress when she returned.

"No problem." She smiled and set down Spencer's credit card with the check and a folded slip of paper. "The person at the booth over there asked me to give this to you." She pointed to a booth a few over from theirs, then frowned, turning back to Rose and Spencer. "Huh, weird. They must have left."

Rose peered at the piece of paper, then her gaze met Spencer's. She reached for the note as Spencer did, their fingers brushing. Her fingertips burned with electricity as Spencer quickly removed his hand from hers. She ignored her burning skin and took the note before he could.

"Who gave you the note? What did they look like?" Spencer asked the waitress as she walked away.

She turned back to face them and paused before responding. "They were wearing a hoodie and sunglasses, which I thought was strange. I don't know how anyone can handle wearing clothing that heavy when it's ninety degrees outside."

"Was it a woman or a man?" Rose asked. "Can you tell us any other details about them?"

The waitress picked up their dishes from the table and started to leave. "Sorry, not really. All I could tell was that it was a man. His voice was deep and kind of husky."

When the waitress was gone, Spencer stared at her intently, like he was waiting for her to talk. But Rose was frozen, rooted to her spot in the sticky, red vinyl booth of the pizza parlor, her mind fixated on the mysterious person with a hoodie and sunglasses. What did they want from her?

Spencer leaned across the table and placed his hand on top of hers.

"Want me to take you home?" he asked in a gentle voice.

"Yeah."

Rose forced herself out of the booth. Spencer grabbed the pizza box, and she followed him to the entrance.

"I have a feeling we'll want to eat this later while we solve the mystery of who The Midnight Flower is," Spencer said.

Rose snorted. "Is that what we're calling them now?"

Spencer held out his hand, and she clasped his hand in hers as they left the restaurant.

"It wasn't *my* idea. I could come up with a much more creative name. It's how they signed the second note, remember?" Spencer said.

"Oh. Right. I guess we need to narrow down the suspects so we can figure out how to stop them."

"We should wait until we're back at your house." Spencer's eyes darted down the sidewalk outside the pizza restaurant. "They might still be here."

Rose followed Spencer to his car. He handed her the pizza, and she held it on her lap.

"What do you think? Who could it be?" Spencer asked, keeping his eyes on the road as he drove.

"Well, all three notes have been left in a public setting, where anyone could have left them . . ." Rose started.

"What's bothering me is how this person knows where you are every day. How do they keep finding you?" Spencer asked.

Rose's fingers clamped down on the pizza box. She hadn't considered that. "I don't know," she whispered.

"Whoever it is, they're intent on hiding their true identity."

"Then there's the weird note from the secret admirer," Rose said.

"It wasn't that weird," Spencer said, his voice suddenly loud.

Rose scrutinized him. "Yeah, it kinda was. Anyway, we still don't know if the secret admirer note is from the same person or if I have two stalkers."

"Either way, I don't think we can rule out your exes, especially since Holly and Reggie were both at Kasey's pool party."

***

Back in her bedroom, Rose scribbled in her notebook, then re-read the names written on their suspect list.

1. *Holly*

2. *Reggie*

Spencer peered over her shoulder. "The problem with it being Holly is that the waitress at Pi Squared said the person who left the note had a deep, husky voice, so it couldn't have been her."

Rose hesitated. "Yeah, but what if she was using a voice changing app?"

Spencer raised his eyebrows. "This is starting to seem more and more like a mystery that's out of our ability to solve. We aren't detectives, Rose. We're just two teens who like to play video games and watch superhero movies." He gestured to her Nintendo Switch lying innocuously on her dresser.

"Don't you think it's weird that Holly was at Kasey's party, though? I can't get past that. Why did she show up? To taunt me and rub it in my face that she's with Reggie now? I'm not sure why she thought I would be jealous."

"Isn't there someone else you're forgetting? That list is awfully short . . ." Spencer prompted.

Rose tapped her pen against her lip. "Who?"

"Uh, Mason . . ."

"What do you mean? I haven't heard from him since summer started.

There's no way it's him." Rose rolled her eyes.

"At this point, I don't think you can rule anyone out." Spencer crossed his arms over his chest. He grabbed the pen from her and added Mason's name to the suspects list.

"Fine. To prove it isn't Mason, I'll text him and make plans to hang out," Rose said stubbornly, getting up from her bed to grab her phone.

"Is that necessary?"

Rose pursed her lips. "You're the one who brought up Mason. I'm trying to narrow it down."

Her fingers swiped across her phone, sending a text to Mason.

> **Rose:** Hey, I haven't heard from you lately. Do you want to hang out tomorrow?

Within seconds, Mason texted her back.

> **Mason:** Absolutely! I'll pick you up at noon?

> **Rose:** Sounds perfect. What do you want to do?

> **Mason:** It's a surprise, but wear comfortable clothes and good walking shoes.

> **Rose:** Okay, see you tomorrow.

Spencer cleared his throat. "Ahem, what's going on?"

Rose turned to face her best friend, panic setting in as it struck her how bold her move had been to make the first move with her crush. "I think I'm going on a date with Mason tomorrow."

Chapter 15: Lily

Six months ago

During the winter, James left the house less and less. Six months had passed since James took her that fateful night in July. How many nights had she cried herself to sleep and prayed for someone to come save her? She didn't think she could go on like this much longer.

Her spirits were lower than ever. Her heart ached for her simple childhood, the innocence she had lost, and all the life experiences she had already missed out on. James had brought her a cupcake on January second, her thirteenth birthday, and he gave her a stack of new paperback books. Lily read the books slowly, savoring each page to make them last because she didn't know when James would give her the privilege of new books again.

When Lily woke up one chilly morning, James was sitting in a chair next to her bed. When he noticed she was awake, he scooted the chair closer and leaned down to kiss her. She let him kiss her—she hadn't kissed him in weeks—and decided to kiss him back. If he was in a good mood, then he might do something nice for her. She held back the urge to gag and wrapped her arms around his neck. James responded by picking her up and pulling her onto his lap so she was straddling him. Lily continued kissing him and ran her hands through his unruly, greasy hair. He must not have showered yet.

"Well, good morning to you too," James said with a chuckle, finally ending the kiss.

"Good morning," Lily replied. She stroked his cheek.

"Someone's in a good mood today. What's gotten into you? I like it." A devilish grin crossed his face.

"I was thinking about how long it's been since we did this," Lily flirted, grinning at him and doing her best sexy impression.

James rolled his eyes. "What do you want?"

Lily feigned shock, pulling slightly back to stare at him. "What do you mean?"

She gazed at him, willing herself not to back down or break eye contact. She couldn't ruin his good mood.

"I know women. You want something, so you're trying to butter me up." He made a rolling motion with his hand, pulled her off his lap, and set her back on the bed. "So, what is it?"

Lily bit her lip. "I want to go to the mall."

James opened his mouth as if he was about to protest.

Lily spoke over him. "I know it sounds stupid, but I miss being able to go shopping and try on clothes in the store. Not that I don't appreciate the clothes you've bought me, but it's fun to pick them out myself. Don't you want to see me model some new outfits?" Lily batted her eyelashes at him.

If he took her to the mall, she could make a run for it and ask someone for help. She might be able to find a security guard and tell them what had happened.

James frowned and stroked the errant dark stubble on his chin that he must have missed shaving. "If I take you to the mall, what do I get out of it?"

Lily swallowed hard. For the dozenth time, she thought about what

Rose would do, but she knew exactly what her tough, smart, resourceful older sister would do. She would do whatever she had to if it meant she could survive.

Chapter 16: Rose

Present day

Brushing her hair up into a high, bouncy ponytail, Rose pulled an elastic around it to hold her wavy, red hair in place. It could be unruly, especially in this heat, so wearing it up was for her own best interest. And Mason's if he didn't want to stare at her with wild, frizzy hair.

Rose smoothed down her leggings and tugged on her tank top, worrying if it was too low-cut. She swiped a little mascara across her eyelashes, added lip gloss to her lips, and checked out her reflection. The doorbell rang, and she yelled for her mom not to answer it.

Of course, she didn't listen, because thirty seconds later, she heard her mom say, "Hello."

She needed to hurry before her mom embarrassed her. Rose reached into her closet to find her sneakers, laced them up, and rushed downstairs. Mason was standing in the doorway leaning against the entryway wall, while her mom grilled him relentlessly.

"Hi!" she said, slightly out of breath from racing down the stairs.

Mason smiled shyly at her. "Hey, Rose. You look pretty."

Rose's mom beamed at the compliment directed toward her daughter. "Don't be out too late. Have fun, kids!"

"Don't worry. I'll have her back home safely in a few hours. It was nice meeting you, Mrs. Blackwood." Mason extended his hand for her mom to shake.

Celia shook his hand, her smile broadening even more—as if that were possible. "Nice meeting you, Mason."

Rose grabbed Mason's hand, opened the front door, and dragged him outside before her mom could get any weirder. She shut the door and tugged Mason toward the truck parked in her driveway. She barely registered that they were holding hands until Mason glanced down at their intertwined fingers and then made eye contact with her.

"Oh, uh, sorry," Rose stuttered, her face flushing as she dropped her hold on his hand.

"I didn't say I didn't like it." Mason smirked and opened the passenger door of his truck for her.

Rose hoisted herself up into the truck and buckled her seatbelt. By the time Mason had pulled out of her driveway, she was floundering. Rose had no clue what to talk about except for The Midnight Flower. But she wasn't sure how to bring that up. It didn't scream "first date conversation," so she would wait until they had hung out a few times. She might as well enjoy going out with the cute guy she had a crush on, even if he was possibly stalking her and blackmailing her with her deepest, darkest secret.

***

Mason stopped the truck in front of a wooded area. Rose noticed a sign that said *Hatcher Garden and Woodland Preserve*.

A dirt trail covered in wood chips led into a cluster of trees. A few other cars were in the parking lot, but Rose didn't see anyone else. The sun was already beating down on them, although it wasn't at full force yet.

Mason pulled a picnic basket and blanket out of the truck bed and gestured for her to follow him.

Her heart thumping with nerves, she joked, "You didn't bring me out here to murder me, right?"

Mason's bright blue eyes widened before he snickered. "Of course not. I wouldn't do that in such a public place."

Her phone buzzed with a text. Rose hastily pulled it out, assuming it was Spencer checking in on her. He had requested updates throughout the date to make sure she was okay. He didn't trust Mason. Rose sent him a quick text telling him where they were and slipped her phone back into her pocket. But Spencer's text had reminded her that she wasn't there to have fun.

Full of anxiety, she gulped and followed Mason down the dirt trail. They passed a small pond with geese swimming and turtles sunbathing on rocks. After the pond, there were various flowers and plants strategically placed to the side of the trail with signs describing each of them.

They walked for a few more minutes until Mason stopped in a clearing. Rose's eyes brightened as she spotted a Little Free Library.

"Did you know this was here?" she asked excitedly, pointing at the cute little wooden house, the shelf inside half-full of books.

"Yup, I thought you might like it. Can we enjoy a picnic first, though?" Mason set the picnic basket on the ground and spread out the blanket. "My lady," he said, beckoning for her to sit. He opened the basket and began pulling out items and placing them on the blanket: sandwiches covered in plastic wrap, a bag of potato chips, and a pasta salad.

"Lunch is served."

"Aww, thanks, Mason. This is so sweet." She smiled appreciatively as she took it all in.

"Sweet enough to make up for not showing at Kasey's pool party?" His blue eyes darted away from her.

"I forgive you. What happened? Did an emergency come up?" Rose asked.

"Yeah, I should have texted you. My mom had to work late, so I had to babysit my little brother. I'm really sorry."

"That's okay. Do you have to babysit a lot?"

"Sometimes. I try to help my mom out as much as I can. Yesterday, I had an interview at Hub City Scoops to work there part-time this summer. I want to help my mom with the bills, so she isn't as stressed," Mason answered.

"Wow, that's nice of you to get a job to help her. I'm sure your mom appreciates it."

Mason shrugged nonchalantly, as if it wasn't a big deal. "She works so hard. If I can make her life a little easier, then I do whatever I can."

Rose thought about her own parents and how hard they worked for her. She could probably find a way to help them too.

"Are you going to eat or what? This is supposed to be a date," Mason said, gesturing to the food.

Rose returned his smile and surveyed the food spread out on the picnic blanket. "Sure, I'm starving."

"Great. I made ham and cheese sandwiches, but there's also some fruit, chips, and pasta salad. And . . ." He pulled out one last container and opened it to reveal the contents. "My mom made us homemade brownies."

"Oh my God, those look amazing! You'll have to tell her thank you from me."

"I will. Trust me, they taste even better than they look," he promised.

They ate in silence. Rose spiraled as the silence stretched between them. *Why isn't he talking? Is it too quiet? Is the date going well? What if he doesn't feel the same? What if he is The Midnight Flower, and this is all an elaborate ruse to get me to trust him? Am I reading too much into it, or—*

Mason interrupted her thoughts with a light chuckle. "You okay? You looked like you were concentrating really hard."

"Oh. Yeah, I'm good. Just thinking about . . . uh . . ." Rose struggled to voice her feelings.

Mason reached out to take her hand in his. "I think I know what you're going to say."

Her insides turned warm and fuzzy. "You do?" She gazed up at him, hoping he had a crush on her too.

"I like you, Rose. I like spending time with you and how you aren't afraid to be yourself. You're courageous and different and special. You aren't like other girls. Plus, you're so pretty." He brushed a stray strand of hair away from her face that had fallen out of her ponytail. "I like you," he repeated.

Rose gasped. That was what the note from the secret admirer said.

"It was you."

"What?" Mason asked.

"You left me an anonymous note," Rose said.

"Oh, uh . . . I can explain."

"You don't have to. I—I like you too, Mason," she said softly, turning away from his intense gaze.

He wasn't going to kiss her, was he? It was only their first date!

But he removed his hand from her face and leaned back, still holding onto her hand. His gaze smoldered, making her too nervous to keep staring into his beautiful blue eyes.

"I'm glad." He let go of her hand and started packing up their picnic. "Do you want to follow the trail for a bit? It doesn't go very far." He turned to her expectantly.

"Sure, that sounds great."

Rose helped him pack up the picnic items, then waited as he carried the basket and blanket back to the car. A minute later, he returned and handed her a water bottle.

"I thought these might be a good idea, especially in this heat," he told her.

"Thanks." She accepted the water and took a few sips until her thirst was quenched.

"Shall we?" Mason held out his hand.

"Can we check out the Little Free Library on our way back?"

"Of course."

Rose wrapped her hand into his, and they set off down the trail. They walked in silence for a few minutes.

"I don't want this to be awkward, but I know about your sister. Lily," Mason blurted out.

Rose froze, her hand tightening its grip on Mason's hand involuntarily.

"Uh, sorry. Maybe that wasn't the right time to mention her. I didn't want you to think I'm an insensitive jerk. I'm sorry about what happened to her," Mason continued.

"What do you mean?" Rose dropped her hand from his and dug her nails into her palms.

"Well, she's been missing for a long time . . ." Mason trailed off, then scratched the back of his neck. "Oh God, I'm an idiot, aren't I? Forget I brought it up. Let's enjoy the rest of the date and go see what books are in that little library thing."

Despite Rose's first-date bliss, she hadn't forgotten about The Midnight Flower and interrogating Mason, but she hadn't wanted to spoil the day. Mason had done that all on his own. She wasn't sure why he had brought up her sister when the date was going so well, but it didn't have anything to do with The Midnight Flower. Mason wasn't capable of doing something so creepy. He was a sweet guy—the type of person who worked to help his mom out, babysat his little brother, and packed a picnic for their date. Would a blackmailing stalker do any of that?

The Midnight Flower had to be someone else.

Chapter 17: Lily

Six months ago

Chest heaving, he lay next to her and grinned. He kissed her on the lips. "I love you, Lily."

"I love you too, James."

"I'm going to go clean up in my bathroom. You should shower too."

"Okay," Lily said.

Lily went into the bathroom and shut the door, turning the lock. She sat on the toilet, her mind racing. Tears came to her eyes, but she swiftly brushed them away. Lily reminded herself that she would do whatever she had to if it meant escaping. She needed to get the hell out of here.

She stepped into the shower, relishing the steaming hot water running over her skin, one of the few enjoyments left in her life. Lily left the bathroom and changed into a different outfit. After she had brushed her hair and dried it, she went into the living room wearing her shoes.

James eyed her shoes. "Going somewhere?" he asked with a sarcastic chuckle.

"Um, y-yes. To the mall?" Lily questioned, unsure of herself.

James shook his head. "You aren't going anywhere. I'll let you order an outfit online if you want new clothes."

"But that was the deal. I thought—" Lily started.

"You thought what? That you could seduce me and then I would do whatever you wanted? Who taught you that trick? Your whore of a sister?" James sneered.

It was the first time he had brought up Rose in months. It hurt to think about her sister. She missed her so much, even if she had been a bitch to her the last time they saw each other. Lily bet Rose regretted it now.

All the hurt, heartache, and loneliness bubbled up inside of her. Lily's bottom lip trembled as her emotions became too much to handle. Her eyes welled with tears, and an anguished cry erupted. The tears poured down her face. She took off her shoes and threw them at the wall, running to the guest room.

"Go to your room!" James shouted with ferocity.

"I already am!" she shouted back.

Lily slammed the bedroom door and stood with her back pressed against it. She slid down to the floor and held her head in her hands. James wouldn't let her out of the house for any reason. She was trapped. Now Lily knew for sure that she could never leave.

Inhaling sharply, she sat still until her breathing steadied and the tears stopped falling. She had to think. She needed a new plan of attack. Lily would convince James that she loved him and wanted to be with him again. If she did as he asked, stopped trying to escape, and he lowered his defenses, she would wait for the perfect opportunity to strike.

If Lily couldn't leave, then the only way to escape was to kill James.

Chapter 18: Rose

Present day

"Rose, please be careful," Spencer pleaded.

"With Mason? Why?" Rose frowned, staring at her best friend and snatching the half-empty bowl of popcorn from him.

"Because! You know why. We still don't have any leads, and he could be—"

"The Midnight Flower?" Rose laughed mirthlessly and shoved a handful of popcorn into her mouth. "It's not Mason, trust me."

"What if he's pretending to like you to get close to you? It could be part of his tactic. It's all a ploy to get you to trust him and tell him the secr—"

"Spencer, you sound ridiculous. Can you please drop it? It's not Mason, I promise. He wouldn't do that to me. He likes me, and I like him. We've been spending a lot of time together lately. I think he's going to ask me to be his girlfriend."

Spencer scooped some popcorn into his mouth. "Okay. If you trust him, then I'll trust you on this. But be careful."

Rose rolled her eyes. "When am I ever *not* careful?"

Spencer snorted. "You? Do I need to remind you of the many dangerous situations you've gotten into? Or rather, that you've dragged me into with you?"

"Yeah, yeah, whatever." Rose scooted forward to the end of her bed, picked up a controller, and handed the second one to Spencer. "Are we going to play *Zombies Attack* or what?"

"Duh." Spencer took the controller from her.

Thirty minutes later, the game wasn't going well.

"Spence, help! I'm getting overpowered!" Rose yelped as a horde of zombies swarmed her on-screen character.

Spencer's character stood there, unmoving. Rose rapidly pressed the "X" button on her controller, slashing through zombies with an ax, but there were too many of them. A zombie lunged at her neck, sinking its teeth into her and tearing into her flesh. Her character fell to the ground and started shaking before turning into a zombie moments later.

The words *GAME OVER* flashed across the TV in a lime-green font. The words exploded and broke apart.

"Thanks for nothing! What were you doing?" Rose glanced over at her best friend to see his controller sitting on the ground.

Spencer was focused on his phone. "Huh?" he asked, setting his phone down and turning to her.

"The hell, dude? I just died. Why didn't you back me up?"

"Oh, sorry. My mom texted me."

Rose's eyebrows scrunched together. "Your mom? What was so important?"

"Uh, she wanted to know if I would be home for dinner," Spencer said, shrugging his shoulders and picking up the controller. "Ready for another round?"

"Are you okay?" Rose asked.

"Yeah, why wouldn't I be?"

"I don't know. You're distracted." Rose grabbed her controller and set up a new game.

"I'm fine, Rose. Don't worry about it," Spencer said, annoyance lacing his tone.

***

After Spencer left, Rose pulled out her notebook with the list of suspects again.

1. *Holly*

2. *Reggie*

3. *Mason*

She chewed on the pen cap as she contemplated who wrote the anonymous notes. It couldn't be Mason. That was as likely as The Midnight Flower being Spencer—which was to say, it was impossible.

When Lily went missing, the police had interviewed everyone they deemed of interest—Rose's family, Spencer and his mom, their neighbors, Lily's teachers, the members of the photography club Lily belonged to, and Rose's friends. Lily didn't have anyone she was close to outside of school, so there weren't many leads for the police to follow.

The Midnight Flower had to be someone Rose hadn't thought of yet. But who else was there? Who would want to scare her and expose her terrible secret?

***

One year ago

Rose met Spencer in the woods behind their houses, the same place they always met whenever she could convince him to sneak out. Sometimes he could be such a baby about it. He worried they would get caught by their parents and get in trouble. Rose, on the other hand, never worried about the consequences. She wanted to have fun and enjoy a little freedom during the summer when they didn't have to go to school every day.

Their freshman year was over, and it was the summer before they started their sophomore year of high school. Rose was excited, but Spencer was nervous about making friends, fitting in, and all that boring stuff. Rose didn't worry about it because Spencer was her best friend, and that had always been enough for her. She didn't care about having a million other friends. Spencer worried too much about what other people thought.

She tiptoed forward and crept behind a giant oak tree that shielded her from the view of anyone walking by. She checked her watch—10:03 p.m. He was late. Her parents had refused to buy her a cell phone until she turned sixteen, so she couldn't contact Spencer to see if he had chickened out.

"Rose?" a voice whispered from the direction of the houses.

"Spence, is that you?" She flicked on her flashlight, illuminating the form of her best friend. "I thought you changed your mind."

Spencer visibly swallowed. "I almost did. I don't know if this is a good idea."

"Come on, this isn't *that* dangerous. We play in the woods all the time."

"Yeah, during the day. It's late. Anything could happen. Plus, our parents think we're at home. They don't know we're out here!" Spencer said in a high-pitched voice.

"Shh, we have to be quiet until we get further into the woods." Rose traipsed through the line of trees, expecting Spencer to follow her.

After a minute of walking, she turned around to make sure he was still behind her. He was.

"What?" he asked when he noticed her staring at him.

"Just making sure you're coming with me."

"I don't want you to do this alone. That's the only reason I'm here," Spencer replied, gritting his teeth. "Let's get this over with."

Rose continued forward until they reached a clearing in the middle of the woods. There was a small circle of bricks surrounding a pile of half-burnt logs from an extinguished fire. Rose propped up her flashlight on one of the bricks and pulled her backpack off of her shoulders. She unzipped her backpack and reached inside.

"Wait!" Spencer said urgently, glancing around the clearing.

"What's wrong?"

"Did you hear leaves rustling?" Spencer asked. "Is someone else here?" he said in a slightly louder voice.

A girl with the same wavy, red hair and green eyes as Rose stepped into the clearing with a flashlight shining on their faces. "Hi," she said sheepishly, remaining on the edge of the clearing.

Spencer's head snapped to meet Rose's eyes. "Did you tell her?"

Rose shook her head. "Why are you here, Lily? Did you tell Mom and Dad that I snuck out?"

Lily bit her lip and stepped closer to them. "No, I promise I won't tell them. I wanted to see what you were doing. Can I hang out with you?"

"No, go home. You shouldn't be out this late," Rose protested.

"But . . . but you're out past our curfew, so why can't I be out too?" Lily's lower lip jutted out, and she crossed her arms over her chest.

"Because you're only twelve. You're too little to be out now," Rose replied.

"You're so mean!" Lily said as tears sprang from her green eyes. She balled her hands into fists by her sides.

Rose's expression softened slightly. "Go home, okay? I'll hang out with you tomorrow. I promise we can do whatever you want."

Lily stormed off without another word.

Spencer turned to Rose when Lily was out of earshot. "Should we go after her and make sure she's okay?"

"No, she'll be fine. Our house is right there." Rose gestured toward their house.

Chapter 19: Lily

Five months ago

Pacing her room, Lily waited for James to wake up. If he was in a good mood, he said goodbye to her before he left for work. The sun was peeking through the curtains in her room, so it had to be past the time when he usually woke up. So why hadn't he come into her room or left the house yet? She would have heard the garage door open if he left. What was going on?

Lily heard the lock click, and the doorknob turned. She hurriedly sat on the edge of her bed and arranged herself casually, grabbing the book from the dresser to pretend she was reading.

"Hello, my perfect flower." James entered the room and stalked toward her, bending down to kiss her on the lips.

"Good morning," Lily responded, doing her best not to gag while she kissed him back.

James joined her on the bed and put his arm around her shoulder. "Do you want to do something fun today? I took the day off of work."

Her mood instantly brightened, considering all the possibilities. "Really?"

James nodded. "We can go to the town an hour away, where no one will recognize us. But I need you to do a favor for me first."

"Okay."

He smiled down at her, pleased at the power he held over her. He pulled out a long, blonde wig from behind his back. "You need to wear this so no one knows who you are. Your beautiful red hair stands out too much." He stroked her hair and pulled her close to him. "Will you do that for me?"

Lily nodded and sank into his chest. She would do whatever he said for the chance to leave the house.

"What made you decide to be spontaneous today?" She smiled up at him, stroking his cheek. She needed more information to plan an escape while they were out of the house.

James kissed the top of her head. "You've been so good the past month, and good girls deserve rewards."

"Thank you," she said softly.

He handed the wig to her. Lily moved in front of the mirror on the dresser and placed the blonde wig on her head. James spent some time helping her arrange it to appear more natural. He had brought bobby pins to hold it in place as well. Then he lifted her chin to force her to look directly at him.

"If I take you out for a fun day, what's in it for me?" he asked.

Lily gulped. She had anticipated that he would ask for something in return. "I'll do whatever you want when we get back."

He shook his head, and his lips set into a grimace. "No, Lily. That isn't what I wanted to hear. You should be eager to please me because it pleases you too. I can tell you're trying, but the lessons still haven't sunk in. I thought you were young enough to be trained to be my perfect flower, but maybe I was wrong about you after all."

James stood from the bed and slapped his hands against his knees. "What a waste of a personal day. I suppose I can go grade some papers." He grinned with a manic smile. "Don't worry. Rose isn't one of my students anymore, so I won't take your impertinence out on her."

Lily's heart ached at the mention of her sister. "Rose . . . how is she? Does she miss me?"

James laughed cruelly. "Miss you? I doubt she's thought twice about you since you've been gone. I'm the only one who cares about you. Your parents and sister didn't search for you. They've moved on with their lives. They're happy you're gone. Remember that, Lily. I did all of this for you, so we could be together at last. Now that we finally have all the time in the world together, don't you want to enjoy it?"

Tears dripped down Lily's cheeks. She wanted to scream at the lost opportunity to leave the house and potentially escape. Her chance of freedom was snatched away.

Breathing deeply, she brushed the tears from her cheeks and stood up. She couldn't let herself continue to wallow. Lily was more determined than ever to leave.

She stalked toward James with purpose and grabbed him by his immaculate dress shirt, standing on her tiptoes to kiss him.

He pulled away from her with a wide-eyed expression on his face. "What are you—"

Lily kissed him again, her lips lingering on his. "I love you, James," she muttered in between kisses.

"Oh, Lily," he moaned as she kissed his neck.

"You're right," she said, distracting him. "I do want to enjoy it."

But she didn't mean what he thought. As they continued kissing, James's kisses became more feverish.

"I hate this wig. You look better as a redhead," he said, yanking it from her head and ripping out the bobby pins.

"Crap!" Lily screamed as the bobby pins tumbled onto the floor.

Thinking quickly, Lily kicked one of the bobby pins under the bed for later. She could definitely use that to do some damage.

Chapter 20: Rose

Present day

"Are you sure you want to eat that?" Mason pointed to the piece of pizza on her plate that she was about to take a bite of.

Her stomach rumbled as the scent of the greasy pizza hit her nostrils. Two slices hadn't been enough of this delicious, cheesy goodness. Rose stuck her tongue out at him. "Yup, it's mine."

Mason smiled and put his hand over hers. "You're lucky I like you."

She responded by taking a gigantic bite of the last slice of pizza.

"I hope you had fun. Do you want to do something else tonight?"

"I was going to hang out with Spencer later." Rose took another bite.

Mason frowned and pulled his hand away from hers. "What are you going to do with Spencer?"

Rose shrugged. "Hang out at my house. Maybe play video games."

"What if I told you that I want to keep hanging out? I'll play video games with you at your house."

Rose fidgeted with her new blouse that Mason had picked out for her. The material was itchy against her skin, and it wasn't her usual style. It was a maroon, scoop-necked, lacy shirt. She preferred T-shirts showcasing her favorite bands and video games. But Mason liked it, so she had worn it on their date.

"I promised Spencer we would hang out. I've been spending a lot of time with you lately, and he's my best friend..."

"Would you rather hang out with him than me? Can't you cancel your plans?" Mason did that Flynn Ryder smolder that made her melt. His dark, curly hair swooped over his left eye perfectly.

Her heart stuttered. "Okay. I'll tell him my plans changed," Rose agreed.

"Good. Let's go."

When they arrived at Rose's house, they went upstairs to her bedroom. Before Rose could set up *Zombies Attack*, Mason examined her desk and picked up the picture of her and Lily. She stared at him uneasily for a second before striding over to him and snatching the picture out of his hand.

"Please don't touch that."

"That's your sister, right? Lily?" Mason asked with a stoic expression on his handsome face.

Rose gritted her teeth. He had to know she didn't want to talk about her sister by now. So, why was he bringing it up?

"Yes," she choked out, holding the picture frame to her chest.

"It's wild what happened to her. I bet you miss her a lot," Mason continued.

Rose set the framed picture gently back in its rightful spot on her desk. "Of course I miss her." Tears sprang to her eyes and her stomach churned. She couldn't deal with this.

Rose went over to her TV stand, rooted around to find two controllers, and handed one to Mason.

Mason gave her a blank expression. "What's this?"

"A controller?" She smirked and picked up the other one. She was annoyed with him for bringing up Lily and was doing her best to distract him from the topic.

Her cell phone rang. She pulled it out of her pocket to see who was calling. *Spencer.* She put the phone on silent and placed it on her desk.

Mason squinted at her. "Who's calling you?"

Rose hesitated before saying, "No one."

He moved closer to her. "Are we really going to play video games when we're alone in your bedroom?"

Rose gulped nervously. "Um, yes? Spencer and I do it all the time."

Mason scoffed and leaned closer to her, their faces mere inches apart. "Yeah, but do you and Spencer do this?"

Mason brushed his lips gently against hers and pulled back to stare at her with the full force of his bright blue eyes.

Rose felt her cheeks warm. "No, he doesn't do that." She wrapped her arms around Mason's neck, clinging to him.

He kissed her again.

A knock came from her bedroom door, and they sprang apart.

"Knock, knock," Rose's dad said, entering her bedroom. "Oh. Hello, Mason. I didn't know you were here." He narrowed his eyes.

Mason waved stupidly as his cheeks flushed. "Hi, Mr. Blackwood."

"Rose, can I speak with you for a minute?" her dad asked.

Mason sprang off the bed and grabbed his cell phone from Rose's desk. "I better get going. I'm sure my mom will want me home to help with my little brother."

Her dad nodded. "Goodnight, Mason."

Rose got off of her bed and walked toward the door, stopping in between Mason and her dad. "Bye, Mason."

Mason left, and her dad advanced further into the bedroom and shut the door.

"What is it, Dad?" Rose asked, her eyes widening with alarm at the expression on her dad's face. She flopped back down onto her bed, grabbing a unicorn stuffed animal to hug to her chest.

Her dad remained standing.

He scratched at his close-cropped, dark brown hair before stopping himself and resting his hands at his sides. "The police found the body of a young girl in the Tyger River. It appears to have been decomposing for some time. She's—she's the right size and age for y-your sister," he choked out before erupting into sobs.

Rose lurched forward to wrap her arms around her dad in a fierce hug. She didn't know what to say, and anything she said at that moment probably wouldn't help. All she could do was sob into her dad's chest, hating herself for not being able to save her sister.

***

The next morning, Rose polished off the rest of her bagel and went to the fridge to search for a drink. As she was rooting around the fridge, the doorbell rang.

"I've got it!" Rose yelled to her parents.

She grabbed a soda and shut the fridge with her hip, bounding to the front door and opening it to reveal her sort-of boyfriend standing on the front steps, looking as handsome as ever. Mason's dark hair artfully swooped over his left eye, and his blue eyes glimmered in the daylight.

"Hey, babe," he greeted her, pulling her close to him for a kiss.

Mason deepened the kiss. She squirmed and tried to get free from his grasp. She didn't want her parents to see them.

"Mason, stop it!" She shoved both hands against his chest.

Mason only tightened his grip on her. He chuckled darkly. "Now that you're finally mine, I'm not letting you get away that easily."

"Excuse me. Why are you talking to my daughter like that? There's a little concept called consent," her dad interrupted in a cold tone.

The front door was ajar. Her dad stood in the house's entryway with his arms crossed over his chest, glaring at Mason.

Rose's face flushed, and she felt her cheeks burning. She extricated herself from Mason's embrace and moved closer to her dad without consciously thinking about it.

"I was joking around, sir. No one was meant to hear that," Mason said.

"I don't care if you were joking or not. I don't like your attitude," her dad responded, looming over them in the doorway.

"Dad, it's fine. We're going to see a movie. I'll be home in a few hours," Rose interjected, grabbing Mason's hand and tugging him down the front steps.

"I don't think so. You're staying home today, Rose," her dad said.

"Why? That isn't fair!" Rose protested.

Mason shrugged his shoulders. "Whatever. I'll text you later."

As soon as he was outside, Rose's dad slammed the door.

"Are you kidding me? Why are you hanging out with a boy who treats you like that?" Her dad stared at her, his hands on his hips in a defensive position. "Does he know I own guns? If he ever touches you again . . ."

"Dad, it's fine. I-I'm handling it."

"I hope you mean you're breaking up with him. Why hasn't Spencer been around here lately? You should hang out with him more," her dad said.

"Yeah, yeah. I'm going to my room," Rose replied.

She locked her bedroom door and picked up a controller, flicking on the TV so she could play *Zombies Attack*. Before, it had been a fun hobby that she shared with Spencer. Now it was becoming her escape from reality.

Rose couldn't help but feel relieved her dad had intervened. After finding out yesterday that Lily's body might have been discovered, she wasn't feeling up to dealing with Mason, anyway. He didn't understand what she was dealing with.

Several hours later, Rose heard a series of knocks on her bedroom door.

"Rose? Are you in there?" her mom called from outside her bedroom.

"Shit," Rose muttered. Then louder, she said, "Yeah, I'm busy."

"Can your dad and I talk to you for a minute?" her mom asked.

"Ugh, fine."

Rose set the controller back down and unlocked her bedroom door, revealing her parents standing beside each other.

"Can we come in?" her dad asked in a gentle tone.

"Sure," Rose said, returning to sit on her bed.

Her parents stood in front of her, her dad's arm wrapped around her mom's shoulder, a united front.

"Rose, I know you like Mason, but we don't think he's good for you. It isn't just about what happened this morning. You've been hanging out with him every day. I can't remember the last time Spencer was over here, not to mention Kasey or any of your other friends. Is—is he treating you okay?" her mom asked tentatively.

"It's fine, Mom. What Dad overheard earlier was a dumb misunderstanding. But don't worry. I'm going to break up with him. So you won't have to worry about him anymore." Rose attempted a smile, but her lower lip trembled.

"I'm sorry, pumpkin." Her dad leaned forward to squeeze her shoulder. "At your age, every relationship feels like the one, but you'll meet someone much better, trust me. Someone who respects you and treats you like the princess you are." He stepped back, eyeing her carefully. "You sure you're okay? Your mom and I are here for you if you need to talk."

Rose shook her head. "No, I'm okay."

Her mom smiled at her with a weak, watery smile. "Okay, then. Dinner will be ready soon. Will Spencer be joining us?"

"Not tonight. And th-thanks for checking on me." Rose hesitated before asking the question that was burning inside of her. "Have you heard any updates . . . about Lily?"

Her mom shook her head and held her fist to her mouth, sobbing.

Her dad squeezed her mom's shoulder and answered, "Not yet, but we'll let you know as soon as we have an update. It's Saturday, and the police said we should know more by Monday."

"Okay," Rose whispered.

Both of her parents hugged her, told her they loved her, and left her room. Rose closed the door and leaned against it, her chest heaving with sobs. Her gaze went to the framed picture of her sister on her desk. The picture she normally avoided looking at but couldn't make herself put away.

Ever since Lily had disappeared, her parents hadn't been the same. She understood why they were protective. With one child gone, all their attention was on Rose. They couldn't bear the thought of anything happening to their remaining child.

Rose attempted to shake away thoughts of her missing sister—well, potentially not missing anymore if it was really Lily's body the police had uncovered in the river. Rose couldn't worry about someone who was already gone. It wouldn't do her any good to feel guilty over what had happened, but the guilt had been eating away at her for the last year, devouring her whole. She flipped the framed photo, so it was face down and plopped onto her bed, nestling her face in a pillow and shutting out the world.

***

"Do you know how embarrassing that was for me? I can't believe you didn't stick up for me in front of your dad. Now he probably thinks I'm a creep." Mason exhaled loudly.

Rose had spent most of the day in her bedroom playing video games alone, but she felt forced to answer when he called later that night.

"I'm sorry you feel that way, but it's my choice if I want you to touch me like that."

"Don't be so dramatic. I didn't do anything wrong," Mason replied.

Rose sniffled. "If you don't know what you did, then I don't want to be with you. I don't think you respect me."

Rose pulled the phone away from her face, doing her best to muffle her cries.

"Are you crying? What did I do wrong?" Mason asked, a mixture of unease and confusion creeping into his voice.

Mason sighed even more loudly when she didn't respond. "I do respect you, Rose. I'm sorry. Is this about your sister? The one-year anniversary is coming up soon, right? That can't be easy."

"Why are you bringing up Lily right now? She has nothing to do with this!" Rose exploded, her emotions welling up inside of her and bursting.

"Okay, okay. Sorry. I thought—"

"Mason, you don't know the first thing about me or Lily," Rose said.

"Fine. If you're going to act that way, I'll text you tomorrow. Give you some time to cool off."

He hung up.

Rose tossed her phone onto her bed, not caring where it landed. She was surer than ever that she needed to break up with Mason. Spencer had been right. Mason wasn't good for her.

Chapter 21: Lily

Four months ago

"James, what do you want for breakfast?" Lily asked, opening the pantry and staring at the contents.

"Pancakes?" he shouted from his bedroom.

"Sounds good!" she yelled back.

Lily pulled the pancake mix and other ingredients from the pantry and started heating the skillet. By the time she was flipping the last pancake, James snuck up behind her and wrapped his arms around her waist. She resisted the urge to scream and pull away. Lily turned around to kiss him, and he greedily kissed her back.

"Thanks for making breakfast, darling." He stroked her cheek with fondness. "This may work out after all. If this continues, you can sleep in my room soon."

Lily bounced on the balls of her feet, excited about the prospect of being able to leave her room more frequently and having more freedom. Because surely that was what he meant. And if so, that meant the potential to escape. All she had to do was wait a bit longer . . .

"Let's eat," James ordered, picking up the plate stacked with pancakes. "Get the maple syrup."

Lily obediently trotted over to the fridge for the maple syrup and set it on the table.

James rewarded her with another kiss. "Thank you."

She sat beside him, and they ate breakfast together, which had become their typical Saturday morning routine. James only worked on weekdays, so they could spend the entire weekend together. Although sometimes he had papers to grade, lessons to plan, meetings with parents, or other teacher responsibilities.

"Shall we watch a movie later? I bought more popcorn and Hershey's bars."

Lily plastered a smile across her face. "My favorite snacks. You're the best."

"Anything to make you happy, Lily."

This was their life now. Over the past month, Lily had adjusted rather quickly to the changes. Her relationship with James was better than ever, or so he thought. Maybe she was becoming a better actress. Nine months had passed, but every day stuck in the house was an eternity.

Chapter 22: Rose

Present day

"How's Mason?" Spencer asked in a sarcastic tone.

Rose's protective shield went up. After having a crush on Mason for months, she didn't want to admit that she had been wrong about him. Yet again, she hadn't been able to see past someone's appearance and determine whether their personalities would mesh well together. She kept walking down the sidewalk, window shopping at the various stores downtown.

"He's fine. Why?" she asked.

Spencer peered at her sideways and pulled down his sunglasses to meet her eyes directly. "Yeah? You've been acting kind of weird lately. We haven't been hanging out much. Did you get another note from The Midnight Flower?"

"No."

"Rose, what's wrong? We've known each other since we were babies. You can tell me anything." Spencer pushed his sunglasses back on, but he remained rooted to the same spot on the sidewalk.

"It's not a big deal. I think I need to break up with—"

As if on cue, Mason walked toward them, his floppy, dark hair flying over his left eye in the slight breeze.

"Rose!" he called with a bright smile that vanished when he spotted Spencer.

"Mason... What are you doing here?" Rose asked, confusion coating her words.

"Getting some new clothes for school." He was carrying several bags over his arm, but he adjusted them so he could hug her.

Rose hugged him back, hoping he wouldn't act weird in front of Spencer.

"What are you two up to?" Mason asked, his blue eyes glancing back and forth between them. He kept his arm possessively around her waist.

Spencer crossed his arms over his chest before he responded. "Window shopping."

"How did you know I was here?" Rose said.

"Obviously, I wanted to surprise my girl." Mason leaned forward, kissing her on the lips and shoving his tongue into her mouth.

Rose pulled away. That didn't answer her question.

"How did you find me?" Rose repeated.

"You checked into downtown Spartanburg when you posted that picture on social media earlier," Mason explained. He leaned forward for another kiss.

Rose used both hands to push him away, but he was relentless. He didn't back off until Spencer intervened.

Spencer laughed awkwardly and backed away from them. "Okay, you two, enough with the PDA. Nice seeing you, Mason."

"Oh, that's too bad. You have to leave?" Mason asked Spencer with a hard glint in his eyes.

Spencer paused and scratched the back of his neck. "Uh, yeah. I should get going." He raised his eyebrows at Rose, as if he was waiting for her to intervene or protest.

"No, wait! Don't go, Spence. Please," Rose said in a small voice.

Spencer turned to her. "Are you sure?"

Rose nodded. Mason finally relinquished his hold on her.

Mason glared at Spencer. "Can't you tell you're not welcome here, dude?"

"Rose asked me to stay, so I'm not going anywhere. *Dude*," Spencer said, balling his hands into fists at his sides.

Mason threw his arms up into the air. "Great. So now I have to hang out with my girlfriend and a third wheel?"

Rose inhaled sharply, gathering her courage to do what needed to be done. "I'm sorry, Mason. It isn't working out." She inched closer to Spencer, who wrapped his arm around her protectively. "Take me home, please?" she asked him.

"Of course," Spencer said, wrapping his fingers around hers like it was the most natural thing in the world.

Mason stood there, staring at them with his mouth hanging open. "Are you kidding me, Rose? You're leaving me for *him*?"

"See, that's the thing, Mason. Good looks aren't enough to make a relationship work. There has to be a connection, common interests, shared beliefs. We don't have any of that," Rose said.

"Whatever. You're going to regret this, Rose Blackwood. I'll make sure of it." Mason stormed off.

Spencer tugged her hand, pulling her down the sidewalk toward his car. "Are you okay? What do you think he meant by that?"

"No, I'm not okay." Rose clenched Spencer's hand. "I haven't wanted to talk about it, but the police found a body in the Tyger River. They said they should know more by tomorrow, but . . . I'm scared, Spence. What if it's Lily?"

"We'll cross that bridge when we come to it. No matter what, I'm always here for you, okay? Don't forget that."

When they were safely in his car, Rose told him all the details about her relationship with Mason—the way he didn't respect her, how he kept bringing up Lily, and even how her parents didn't like him.

The puzzle pieces were connecting. In the beginning, Mason had fooled her into thinking he was a sweet guy—caring, romantic, and kind. But the real Mason wasn't like that at all. In fact, he seemed to be the exact opposite.

Spencer had been right not to trust him. The Midnight Flower hadn't crossed her mind in weeks, but now the anonymous person's identity consumed her again. If they were intent on getting revenge...

The most likely suspect was Mason.

***

Rose tossed another handful of M&Ms into her mouth, then felt a piece of candy pelt the side of her head.

"Ow!" She turned to glare at Kasey.

"Ow?" Kasey questioned, raising an eyebrow. "Really?"

"It was my knee-jerk reaction." Rose rolled her eyes and shoved the bowl full of popcorn and M&Ms away from Kasey. "How was the cruise?"

Kasey's eyes lit up. "So much fun! The Bahamas were beautiful. Ten out of ten would recommend."

"What did you do the whole time you were on the boat? It sounds kind of boring to me."

Kasey giggled. "Um... actually, I met a guy."

Rose gasped and leaned closer to her friend for the gossip. "Ooh. What's his name? What's he like?"

"His name is Jorge. He's from Brazil, and he's gorgeous. We spent most of the week together. When I was leaving, he kissed me." Kasey's cheeks flushed, and she turned away from Rose.

"Aww, Kasey, that's so great! Does he live in America? Will you get to see him again?" Rose knew it was Kasey's first kiss, and she was excited for her.

"Yeah, but he lives in California. He's a foreign exchange student. We exchanged phone numbers. We even talked about meeting up over winter break, but we'll see what happens. I don't want to get my hopes up." Kasey bit her lip.

"You totally deserve to get your hopes up. He sounds great." Rose smiled sadly, her mind drifting to her nonexistent relationship. Yet again, she was single.

"Well, how's Mason?" Kasey's eyes twinkled with mischief as she bumped her shoulder.

Rose shook her head. "Not what I thought he was. He keeps asking about Lily," Rose choked out in a whisper.

"What? Why?" Kasey asked sharply, straightening from her slouched position on the black leather couch.

Rose shrugged. "I guess he might be interested in what happened to her because nothing exciting happens in our small town. He doesn't respect me, either. He keeps trying to force me into things I don't want to do. I don't think he really cares about me."

"Oh, Rose, I'm sorry. There will be other boys, though." Kasey giggled, then corrected herself, "Or girls."

"I know."

The weird thing was, when Kasey mentioned other boys, an image of a sweet guy with charming hazel eyes and curly, light brown hair popped into her head. Why was she thinking about Spencer at a time like this? He was her best friend—nothing more.

Kasey leaned in to hug her. Rose wrapped her arms around her friend.

When Kasey pulled back, she asked, "You're really quiet all of a sudden. What are you thinking about? Someone else you have your eye on?"

"Nah, I'm just excited about this movie." Rose pressed play on the remote, dropping the subject. That was a dangerous road to go down, and she already had enough of those in her life.

Chapter 23: Lily

Two months ago

"What do we think about Rose?" James asked with a stern expression on his face.

"Rose is a whore who uses her looks to get what she wants. She doesn't care about anyone but herself. She won't amount to anything. She deserves everything she gets. And she'll never know true love, not like what we have," Lily replied, reciting the words James had trained her to say.

The last part was her own addition, though. An authentic smile crossed James's face. He was so handsome when he smiled like that. A glimmer of what she used to feel for him flickered inside her. She reminded herself that he was a monster who had kidnapped her and was holding her hostage—he had used his appearance, position, and charm for evil.

He kissed her on the cheek. "That's my girl. I'm proud of you."

James wrapped his arms around her and squeezed her tightly. He flipped on the TV and scrolled through the channels until he found a movie they agreed on.

"This is perfect," Lily whispered, nuzzling into his neck.

It was the opposite of perfect—it was a nightmare—but at least she could watch a movie tonight.

"I agree. This is what I've always wanted."

"Me too," Lily replied. She curled up her legs on the couch and laid her head on his chest. She listened to his heart beat, wondering what it would take to make it stop beating.

***

Lily awoke with a start to a dark room. She felt around her, touching silken sheets and a quilt, assuming she had fallen asleep during the movie and James had carried her into her room. But, wait, that couldn't be right. The sheets in her bed weren't silk.

As her eyes adjusted, she became confused. She didn't recognize the room. The wall across from the bed had a TV mounted on it, and the bathroom was on the right side of the room instead of the left. Was she in his bedroom?

Still half asleep, she clambered out of bed and peeked into the bathroom. It was much more spacious than the one in her room. James must have updated it at some point. Double pedestal sinks were in front of a large, ornate mirror, and a gigantic soaker tub stood in the corner. Where was he?

Rubbing her eyes, Lily left the bedroom, heading down the hall to the family room. She heard James's raised voice and realized he must be talking on the phone.

The only words she could make out were, "Well, you better fucking fix it because I'm not going to jail over your mistake!"

She figured it was best to ignore his heated conversation, so she tiptoed down the hall, heading to the front door. This was it. She could make it out while he was distracted and—

James's hand grasped her shoulder, forcing her to turn around. "What are you doing out here?" he snarled.

"I woke up and wasn't sure where I was. I came out here to find you." Lily wrapped her arms around his waist. "Is everything okay? It sounded like you were arguing with someone."

"Oh, yes, my perfect flower. Never mind about that. Everything is wonderful." James scooped her up into his arms and carried her back to the main bedroom.

He set her gently on the bed and settled in next to her, draping his arm around her waist, ensuring she couldn't slip out of bed without him noticing. Lily wanted to believe him, but she knew what she had heard. She didn't think she could fall asleep again.

Why would James go to jail? What had he done?

Chapter 24: Rose

Present day

Rose pulled her mom's car into the parking lot of the coffee shop, Spill the Beans, and shifted into park.

She slung her wristlet around her wrist and locked the car, heading to the coffee shop. She was focusing on checking her phone for texts from Spencer and not paying attention to where she was going when she stumbled into a solid form.

"Oh God, I'm so sorry!" she stuttered, her eyes darting up to meet the eyes of the unfortunate person she had run into.

The prettiest green eyes she had ever seen stared back at her, taking away her breath. She spotted shoulder-length, dark brown hair and admired a leather jacket covering a muscular body. She hadn't expected to see her ex-boyfriend, Kylar.

"Hi, Rose," he said in a scratchy voice. He cleared his throat. "Sorry I sound like crap. I'm getting over a cold."

"Uh, hi. How are you?" she asked awkwardly.

Rose was sure her face was bright red after gawking at her ex.

"I'm okay." He squinted as if he was scrutinizing her. "Are you?"

"Yup. Yeah. I'm good."

"Okay."

"Sorry, I'm meeting someone." She pointed to the inside of the coffee shop. "He's probably already waiting for me. I'm running late."

It was a lie, but she would have said anything to escape the situation. Rose was only there to get coffee for herself and Spencer. Afterward, she planned to go over to his house to apologize for how she had pushed him away while dating Mason. She wasn't sure if he was mad at her, but she needed to mend their friendship—relationship—whatever it was.

"Okay. See you later," Kylar said, turning to walk away.

Well, that was weird.

Rose opened the door to the coffee shop and shot for the counter to order a drink. She didn't like coffee that much, but she could order a fancy coffee drink with whipped cream and chocolate syrup. Anything to drown out the coffee taste. Spencer loved café au laits, so that's what she ordered for him.

Someone tapped on her shoulder, and Rose whipped around, on edge after her run-in with Kylar.

An elderly man smiled at her. "Excuse me, miss. I think you dropped this. It fell out of your purse."

"No, I don't think I dropped anything," Rose said, turning back around dismissively.

"Is your name Rose?" the old man asked. "That's who the note is addressed to."

"Um, yes, thanks." Rose snatched the folded piece of notebook paper from him and shoved it into her wristlet.

But she had seen a glimpse of the handwriting, and she knew who the note was from.

Who else could have slipped a note into her wristlet? It had to be Kylar. He hadn't even been on her radar until now. The only question was, how had he known she would be there?

***

Spencer sipped his café au lait. "Ah, this is so good." He smirked knowingly at her. "Why did you bring me coffee from my favorite coffee shop? Do you need a favor? You know I'll do anything for you. You don't need to bribe me."

A smile spread across her face, the first genuine smile she had worn in weeks. She put her hand on his arm. "I know, and I appreciate that more than you'll ever understand."

Spencer gaped at her hand on his arm, then his eyes went back to her face. "Rose, what's going on? You're kind of freaking me out."

"I ran in to Kylar at the coffee shop." Rose opened her wristlet and pulled out the newest note. "This has to be from him."

"Whoa, what? Now you think Kylar is The Midnight Flower?" Spencer asked, his eyebrows scrunching together in confusion. He set his coffee on the rickety table in his bedroom.

"I know we didn't consider him, but he's a suspect. I'll add him to my list when I get home," Rose said, taking a sip of her expensive coffee milkshake.

"Hmm, okay. I wish I had been there with you." Spencer snuggled into her side and rested his head on her shoulder.

Rose let him, feeling at ease with her best friend by her side. "Why?"

"Because I—" Spencer started.

"Spence! Is Rose in there with you? Her mom called and wants to know why she isn't answering her phone," Spencer's mom called from down the hall.

"Yeah, sorry. She'll call her back!" Spencer yelled to his mom.

Rose pulled out her phone and saw the three missed calls. "Shit. I should probably go home and see what she wants. Text me later?"

"Of course," Spencer said.

He always walked her to the door when she left, but this time, they had somehow ended up holding hands. Rose couldn't remember who had initiated it. All she knew was that nothing had ever felt like this. Her fingers tingled as he squeezed her hand and said goodbye.

"Bye, Spence," she replied, throwing her arms around his neck.

***

When Rose arrived at home, her parents were both sitting on the couch waiting for her. *Uh oh. This can't be good.*

"What's going on?" she asked, sitting on one of the armchairs across from the couch.

"Hi, pumpkin. We're glad you're home. The police called. They performed an autopsy on the body they found," her dad explained.

"Oh my God. So . . . ." Rose said, unable to force herself to ask the question she wanted to.

Is it Lily?

Tears slid down her mom's cheeks as she sobbed uncontrollably. "It isn't her. It isn't Lily."

"Melanie Powell. A fourteen-year-old girl who went missing two years ago," her dad added.

"So Lily could still be alive," Rose interjected, her heart nearly bursting full of hope.

Chapter 25: Lily

One month ago

"Remember, Lily, don't leave the house and don't go into my office," James repeated. "I'm trusting you."

Lily threw her arms around his neck and stood on her tiptoes to kiss him. Excitement pulsed throughout her body. She could barely contain it, but she needed to, so he didn't suspect anything was amiss.

He chuckled and kissed her back. "I left a new puzzle for you in the living room if you get bored. Please don't forget to have dinner ready by the time I get home," James told her.

"I will, James. Have a good day at work. I love you!" Lily said as James left the house.

"I love you too!" he yelled from outside.

Sitting cross-legged on the rug in the family room, Lily worked on a puzzle. She planned to wait ten minutes to ensure he was really gone. It was the first time he had let her freely roam the house while home alone. The two warnings he had reiterated to her were to not leave the house and to not go into his office. Of course, she had tried to get into his office after he left that day, but the door was locked and she couldn't find the key.

After eleven months of living with James, the constant thought in her mind was about how she could leave. In her old life, Lily didn't have any friends. She never had a boyfriend. Her parents and sister didn't pay attention to her. Rose was the one always getting into trouble, so their parents worried about her all the time. Lily was the perfect child who did nothing wrong. Her parents stopped worrying about what she was doing. They stopped checking in and making sure she was okay, and that's when she had met James.

But now, she was trapped in this house with the man she had thought she loved. Today she planned to leave.

James promised that after she turned eighteen, they would get married. That was a while away, though, as she had just turned thirteen in January. Before that, he needed to save more money. But he told her they would change their names and move somewhere far away, maybe even leave the country. Lily had gone along with his plans, pretending that was the future she wanted too. She had to pretend so she could survive.

Lily heard the doorbell ring and froze after jiggling the office doorknob for the second time. Her gaze went to the front door, which was solid oak and didn't have a peephole, so she couldn't see who was there. She cautiously moved down the hallway and toward the front door. The doorbell rang again.

With shaking hands, she reached for the deadbolts and unlatched both of them. This was it. Her chance to escape. She opened the door to reveal a petite, blonde teenager.

The girl's ice-blue eyes widened when they made eye contact. "Lily?"

Lily stared at the familiar face for a moment, letting it sink in. She had so many questions.

"Holly? What are you doing here?" Lily asked, squinting her green eyes in confusion.

"I came here to talk to Ja—Mr. Mortensen. Fuck, Lily, why are you here?" Holly asked, trying to peer into the house. "Is he home?"

Lily shook her head and grabbed Holly's hand. "Quick, get inside now before someone sees you."

Lily pulled Holly inside and slammed the door. "You have to help me get out of here. James kidnapped me last summer, and he's been holding me hostage here."

Holly gasped and placed both hands over her mouth. "Oh my God, Lily! You've been here this whole time? Why did he take you? I can't believe—"

"There's no time to explain. Can you bring me home? I need to leave while he's gone." Lily reached for the doorknob.

Holly held her palm out in a 'stop' gesture. "Wait, there's something I have to tell you first. Have you heard of The Midnight Flower?"

Lily shook her head. "Who is that?"

"This will take too long to explain, but I swear, I didn't know Mr. Mortensen was the one who kidnapped you. I'm working with him on . . . something else. I promise I'll help you get out."

Lily crossed her arms over her chest. "I'm not stupid. You're up to something. Why else would you be at the house of your former teacher? I don't know if I should trust you. Are you and Rose still together?"

Lily had missed out on so much while being trapped there. It felt weird not knowing who her own sister was dating.

Holly sighed and rubbed her face. "No, she broke up with me in August. There's something I have to tell you, though. I know the truth about the night you disappeared. About how Rose and Spencer saw you that night and told you to go home."

"She . . . she told you about that? Then why haven't the police found me?" Lily's voice became high-pitched.

Holly bit her lip and dropped her gaze to the ground. "Rose didn't want to get in trouble. The more time that passed, the worse it would have been for her to come clean with what really happened. I'm the only one she told about seeing you before you disappeared. She trusted me with the truth. But the guilt has been eating her alive for the past year. She regrets not walking you home, not telling your parents what happened—all of it. You have to believe me, Lily. All Rose wants is to find you."

"If she told you all that, then she must have really trusted you. We need to come up with a plan while James is at work. But first, tell me about The Midnight Flower. I need all the information I can get," Lily said.

Chapter 26: Rose

Present day

Spencer snuggled against her side, resting his head on her shoulder. "I wish you would have told me sooner how Mason was treating you," he said softly. "I would have punched his lights out."

Rose shook her head. "I was embarrassed. I wish I hadn't trusted him, though. He didn't like us hanging out. I think he was jealous of our friendship."

"Red flag number one: when your boyfriend doesn't let you hang out with other guys, especially when they've been your best friend for your entire life," Spencer said.

Rose groaned and pushed Spencer off her shoulder. "I know. I was stupid to think he liked me."

"Hey, stop it. You aren't stupid. He's the idiot to have messed up his chance with you. You're the most beautiful girl I've ever seen. You're special. Everywhere you go, you leave a trail of light, no matter how dark it seems. If I were dating you, I would never treat you so badly."

The words hung heavily in the air between them. Spencer swallowed and his eyes darted away from her, then quickly back to her face again.

"Spence?"

"Yeah?"

"Do you really mean that?" Rose focused on him inquisitively, pondering the relationship she had never let herself consider.

It wasn't that she had never seen Spencer that way—it used to be all she thought about. But since he never made a move, she had assumed he only wanted to be friends. She had dated other people and tried to forget about having feelings for him. In fact, it might have been the exact reason she kept dating other people who were so different from him and so wrong for her. Now she only wished he had spoken up sooner.

"If I mean it, what would your response be?" Spencer dropped his eyes to the worn carpet.

Rose leaned forward to press her lips softly against his cheek. "This."

Spencer turned his head to face her, his eyes wide with wonder. Rose smiled and backed away, clasping her hand in his.

"Let's take it slow, okay? I need some time to sort out my feelings. My relationship with Mason was . . . a mess."

Spencer pursed his lips, but he nodded. "Of course, whatever you need. I just want you to be happy."

Rose smiled the sad smile of someone who hadn't felt truly happy in more than a year. "Someday, I hope I'm happy again too."

Spencer paused as recognition dawned on his face. "Are you thinking about—"

"Yeah." Rose didn't need to say another word. Spencer had been there for every important moment—and most of the insignificant moments too—so he just knew.

***

One year ago

Giggling, Rose pulled a half-empty bottle of rum from her backpack. Spencer's eyes widened, and he rushed toward her.

"What are you doing with that? Is that *alcohol*?"

Rose rolled her eyes. "You know what it is. It's the special bottle my dad keeps in his nightstand drawer."

"How did you sneak that out?"

Rose shrugged and unscrewed the cap. "It wasn't that hard. I snuck into my parents' bedroom when my dad was at work today. My mom went grocery shopping, and I was babysitting Lily."

"Did Lily see you take it?" Spencer asked worriedly.

"Nah, but if she did, she won't tell them. She cares what I think about her too much, so she won't want to piss me off."

Tipping the bottle back, Rose sipped the rum, feeling the burning sensation as it slid down her throat. She did her best not to react, wanting to impress Spencer.

"Wow." She smacked her lips together.

"What? Is it good?" Spencer squinted at her.

"Here, try some." Rose thrust the rum bottle into his face.

"I don't know . . ."

"Please," she pouted. "Do it for me? It's no fun drinking and breaking the rules by myself. I need my best friend to join me."

"If you insist." Spencer took a huge swig, probably trying to impress her too, but he ended up coughing and spitting out half of it before swallowing.

Rose giggled and put her hand over her mouth. "What do you think?"

Spencer coughed again. His eyes watered. "It . . . burns . . ."

"Just a little." She teased him and took the bottle back. As she sipped more of the amber liquid, warmth spread throughout her body.

Spencer checked the watch on his right wrist, then showed her the time. "It's almost eleven. Should we go home now?"

"Not yet. I want to stay out until midnight."

"Fine, but I'm not doing this because I condone it. I'm only staying so you aren't out here by yourself in the middle of the woods so late."

"Thanks for worrying about my safety." She grinned cheekily at him.

Spencer rolled his eyes, but he smiled back and took the rum from her, this time taking a few slow, small sips. "I worry about your sanity too, so don't flatter yourself."

Chapter 27: Lily

One month ago

When James returned home from work, Lily greeted him at the door. She had left her hair down—the way James liked it—instead of throwing it into her usual messy ponytail. She waited for him to notice or compliment her, but he didn't.

Lily kissed him on the cheek. "How was your day?" She took his satchel from him and set it on the table in the entryway.

James grumbled an incoherent reply and entered the kitchen, fishing around in the pantry until he pulled out a bottle of whiskey. He poured some into a glass.

"Are you okay?"

He took a long sip of his drink. "Yes, Lily, just peachy. Why wouldn't I be?"

"I don't know. You seem upset," Lily said.

"Did anyone come to the house today?" James paused in sipping his whiskey and set the glass on the counter. He stalked toward her, and his face hovered inches from hers.

"No. No one was here," Lily lied.

Lily's knees became weak. Her heart beat harder in her chest. How did he know? What if Holly had lied to her? But there was no way Holly could have known the truth about the night Lily disappeared without Rose telling her... She had to trust Holly.

James's shoulders lowered slightly, and he picked up his whiskey glass again. "Okay, okay. That's good. I believe you."

Lily tilted her head sideways. "Were you expecting someone? Because you were at work, so why would—"

"No, no, not at all. I thought one of my friends was going to stop by today, but I must have remembered the day wrong," James replied, sipping his whiskey again.

"James..." Lily put her fist to her mouth, resisting the urge to bite her nails. James hated when she did that.

"Yes, my perfect flower?" His tone turned sickly sweet, putting her on edge.

But this was her best shot. Holly was coming back for her, and in the meantime, she was going to push James as much as possible.

"Why did you pick me?" she asked.

"What on earth are you talking about?"

"I mean, why me? What was it that made you choose me over all the other girls at school? You were with Rose first, weren't you? Was that a coincidence?" Lily asked, feigning innocence.

"What are you implying? You think I planned this from the start?" he snarled. He set his whiskey glass on the kitchen counter and loomed over her.

Lily prepared herself for whatever the consequences would be. "Are you The Midnight Flower?"

James stumbled backward several steps, as if she had landed a physical blow on him. He held his hand to his chest. "Where did you hear that name? Who have you been talking to?"

"Tell me the truth, James. Have you been terrorizing Rose and stalking her the whole time I've been here? Are you trying to lure her here to save me, so you can be with her instead?" Lily questioned, her voice becoming louder and louder.

"That's enough!" James shouted, slapping her across the face with so much force that Lily clung to the counter so she didn't fall.

"Why would I want to be with that whore?" James asked, clearly speaking to himself. "Rose is nothing to me. I can have any girl I want," he muttered.

Lily gazed at him, batting her eyelashes. "But I thought I was the love of your life, so why does it matter if you can have any girl?"

"Because power matters. What's the point if you aren't the one in control?"

"You aren't in control, though. I don't love you anymore," Lily replied coolly, inching toward the guest room.

"I'll make you regret saying that. I chose you out of all the girls at your school, and this is how you repay me? After all I've done for you. All I've sacrificed. I've given you everything I have. Besides, no one misses you. They barely notice you're gone."

"My family hasn't given up. They'll find me. I know they will," Lily said.

James sneered. "No one is searching for you. I've told you that time and time again. You're staying here with me. Forever."

Chapter 28: Rose

Present day

After she finished telling him what had happened at the coffee shop, Spencer's eyes narrowed. "You know Kylar and Mason could be working together, right?"

Rose pushed her wavy, red hair behind her ears. "Yes. Here." She pulled the latest note out of her wristlet and shoved it toward Spencer.

"Have you read it yet?" he asked.

"No, I waited so we could read it together."

He unfolded the note, laying it out on the desk in her bedroom next to the other two notes.

Rose,

You think you're so clever and that you'll get away with your crimes, but the worst crime of all was that you broke my heart. I promise you'll regret it. Tell your parents and the police the truth about that night, or I'll do it for you.

The Midnight Flower

Rose gulped and read the note again. "Okay, now I'm not so sure it's either of them."

"Wait..." Spencer picked up the note and silently mouthed the words as he read it again. "Let's think this through logically. I didn't think Kylar was so petty. I mean, he wasn't my favorite person, but out of all the people you dated, he wasn't the worst. Not the type I would imagine doing this."

"Me neither. I didn't think he was capable of this, but if I really broke his heart—"

Spencer put his arm around her and squeezed her shoulder before he said his next bitter words. "Then he wants revenge. And some people will do anything to get what they think they deserve."

***

Later in the week, Spencer placed a tin into her hands. "Here. My mom made homemade chocolate chip cookies for you."

"Aww, tell her I said thank you. Those are my favorite." Rose smiled and set the cookie tin on the kitchen counter.

"I know. That's why I brought them over." Spencer raised an eyebrow. "You aren't going to open them and eat half the cookies before your dad can steal them?"

Rose shrugged and stared longingly at the cookies. "I ate a big breakfast. I'll eat them later."

Spencer's eyes widened incredulously. "I've never seen you turn down a cookie, no matter how much you've eaten. Are you feeling okay? Are you sick?"

She fought the frown forcing its way across her face, wanting to tell Spencer the truth about how she hadn't been sleeping or eating much lately since the police discovered the young girl's body in the Tyger River. It could have been Lily, but it wasn't.

Rose couldn't help but wonder what had happened to her sister. She didn't think she would feel okay again until she knew for sure if she was still alive. But she also didn't want to discuss it. Spencer would do his best friend duty and try to comfort her, but it would be for nothing. The only thing that could ease her guilt would be if Lily was found alive.

"I'm fine. Promise."

"Okay. What are we doing today?" Spencer leaned against the counter and stared at her with a small smile on his face.

Scrunching up her nose, she tried not to think about the gooey, freshly baked chocolate chip cookies sitting in front of her. The scent of the baked goods filled the kitchen, teasing her. Her stomach churned uncomfortably.

"Video games?"

"Sure. Do you . . . um . . . I mean, can we—"

Rose laughed. "Was that a complete sentence?"

Spencer adjusted the collar on his polo shirt—a weird outfit choice for what was supposed to be a chill day hanging out. "I was wondering if you wanted to go out. Like, on a date."

Rose punched him lightly on the arm. "I would love to."

Spencer rubbed his arm where she had punched him and winced, pretending it hurt. "If you don't kill me first."

Rose laughed again and stepped closer to him, so their faces were inches apart. She wrapped her arms around his waist and nestled her head into his chest. Spencer entwined his fingers in her hair and stroked the top of her head. He was so gentle with her, so careful and respectful of her feelings. She sighed happily. She still wanted to take it slow with him, but she could get used to this.

Her dad cleared his throat, interrupting their moment. "What's going on in here?"

Rose shoved Spencer away from her, and he responded by taking an unnecessary number of steps back.

"Nothing," Rose told her dad.

All they had done was hug, after all. They had been best friends for their entire lives, so the number of times they had hugged was infinite. But Rose knew they had never hugged like that before.

Her dad raised an eyebrow and strolled into the kitchen. "Hello, Spencer. We've missed seeing you around here. How's your summer going?"

"Great. It's been great, Charlie."

Spencer had known her parents long enough to be on a first-name basis with them, unlike Mason, who had called her parents "sir" and "ma'am."

Her dad pointed to the cookie tin on the counter. "Are those cookies from your mom?" he asked Spencer.

"Yup," Spencer said. "Freshly baked this morning."

"Oh, boy," her dad said, pulling the lid off the container and popping a cookie into his mouth.

"Dad!" Rose chided. "His mom made those for me."

"Oh." Her dad snagged two more cookies, then put the lid back on the cookie tin. "Well, I'll only take a few more then." He snickered and left the room, holding the stack of cookies in his hand while he munched on the first one.

Rose pouted.

Spencer laughed and grabbed a cookie from the tin with his hazel eyes glistening at her as he did so. "Your dad had the right idea."

Rose took a cookie for herself. "Oh, fine. I guess I better eat one before everyone else does."

"Good idea. So, did you think of what else you want to do today?"

Rose peered around the corner into the hall, on the lookout for her dad. "Let's go upstairs to my room." She grabbed his hand and yanked him up the stairs, then shut her door.

"Rose, are you alone in there?" her mom yelled from outside her bedroom door a minute later.

Spencer peered at her with a terrified expression. He still clasped her hand and let go when he realized it.

Her mom pounded on the door. "Rose?"

"Let her in! She's going to think we're doing something!" Spencer said.

Rose giggled. "You wish."

Rose turned the doorknob to see her mom standing there with a raised fist as if she was about to knock again. "What's up?"

Her mom crossed her arms over her chest, a smirk playing across her face. "What are you two doing in there?"

"Playing video games," Spencer blurted out before Rose could answer. Rose nodded.

"That's it? Then why did your dad catch you two canoodling in the kitchen?"

Spencer's face paled, and a grimace overpowered it. He opened his mouth, but Rose cut in before he could give an incriminating answer.

"We were just hugging, Mom. Besides, we always hang out in my room with the door shut. Since when do you care?"

"Uh-huh." Her mom's eyes narrowed. "You broke up with Mason five days ago. And you're happier than you have been all summer. I was talking to Fiona on the phone because she's noticed a change in Spencer's behavior too. Are you two . . . dating?"

"*Ugh, Mom*! It was a hug. I was going to talk to you later, but since you asked, yes, we're dating."

Spencer turned to her, leaned close, and put his arm around her shoulders. "We are?"

Rose's face flushed. "Well, we are, aren't we?"

Her mom chuckled and turned to leave. "I'll leave you two alone to figure it out. I'll see you later."

Rose shut the door again and retreated into her room with Spencer following behind her. She sat on her bed, sinking into the comfort of her safe space. "Well . . ."

"Rose, you know I like y—" Spencer started.

Rose's phone rang, interrupting the conversation. Rose raced over to her desk to pick it up and answered without checking the caller ID or thinking twice about it.

"Hi, Rose. I'm glad you answered. I didn't know if you would."

"Mason?" Rose questioned.

Spencer shook his head, but she ignored him.

"Can we talk?" Mason said. "There's something I need to tell you."

"What is there to talk about? We're done, Mason."

"It's about the note in your bag."

"I know either you or Kylar put it there! And I know you're The Midnight Flower!" Rose screamed.

"What are you talking about? The Midnight *what*?" Mason questioned.

Spencer signaled for her to hang up the phone, but she kept talking, unable to stop once she started.

"I broke up with you because we were terrible together. You have a weird obsession with my sister, and I'm not sure why. We have nothing in common, and you didn't respect me or treat me the way I deserve. I'm dating Spencer now, so leave me alone," she finished, ending the phone call in an angry huff.

Rose threw her phone onto her bed and sank into the mountain of pillows. Spencer joined her on the bed and sighed.

"You have no self-control, Rose," he joked, putting his hand on her leg and sending tingles throughout her body.

Smirking, her eyes lingered on his lips. "How much do you want to bet on that?"

Chapter 29: Lily

One month ago

James grabbed her by the arm and shoved her into the guest room. "Stay in there until I come get you."

"But, James!" she protested. "What did I do?"

He glowered at her, his eyes darkening. "You know what you did. You get in too much trouble when you have freedom. You think you can get away with doing whatever you want, saying whatever you want. You'll do as I say from now on. Stay in this room until you prove your love for me. Only good girls get rewards."

It was the third time James had left Lily in the guest room for more than a day without bringing her food or water—although at least she had the bathroom sink for water when she got thirsty. James had punished her after every escape attempt. She was already becoming weak. If he came into the room, she would probably do whatever he asked to be able to eat something. That thought terrified her.

Had she been wrong to trust her sister's ex? Had she missed her one opportunity to leave?

Panic crawled up Lily's throat, threatening to choke her. *No, this isn't it. It can't be.* She had survived for eleven months—she sure as hell wasn't giving up now. Lily climbed back into bed, staring at the same four walls she had stared at for eleven months. Almost a year since she left home.

It was June. School had ended for the year. Rose would be at home most days, hanging out with Spencer and getting into trouble most likely.

Lily wondered if she would ever see her parents and Rose again. Heck, she even wanted to see Spencer and his mom at this point. Anyone but James and his stupid, handsome face.

As she lay in bed with the blanket drawn up to her chin, feeling dizzy from hunger, she heard voices coming from down the hall.

Voices? Someone else is in the house!

Quietly, Lily crept out of the bed and tiptoed over to the door, pressing her ear up against it. She strained against the door, listening for the voices. Soon, they started talking again. One of them was James, but the other voice didn't sound familiar. It was a deep voice, another man, but who was it?

Lily pondered what to do. Just because James had someone over, that didn't mean they would help her. Holly had told her all about The Midnight Flower and his lackeys. For all she knew, they were all helping James get away with keeping her there. She debated screaming or yelling for help, but she stayed quiet and waited.

She heard the stranger chuckling, and James responded. Then the doorbell rang. This time, a third voice joined in, a voice Lily would recognize anywhere. She had known him since birth.

Chapter 30: Rose

Freshman year – December

"Mr. Mortensen, I hope you have a good Christmas!" Rose said, waving to him as she said goodbye.

Her English teacher was young, and most of the girls in her grade had a crush on him. With his jet-black hair, kind, green eyes, and tall, muscular figure, he was an attractive man. It didn't hurt that he was much younger than most of the teachers at their school. Rose guessed he was only in his early twenties. Like the other girls in her class, she had a crush on him.

"Rose, could you come here for a minute, please?" Mr. Mortensen asked.

"Sure." She sauntered up to his desk as her classmates filed out of the room. She waved to Spencer, reassuring him that she would catch up to him later.

Mr. Mortensen sat at his impressively large desk, his legs crossed at the ankle. He gestured for her to sit in the chair across from him, then folded his hands on top of the desk and leaned toward her.

The classroom was empty now.

"Rose, I think you're much farther ahead of your classmates. You're a smart girl." He smiled at her, exposing his white teeth in a friendly grin.

Rose blushed and scratched at her neck nervously. "Thanks, Mr. Mortensen."

"You don't have to call me that. School's out for two weeks. Call me James." He winked at her and stood from his desk.

She smiled at him cheekily. "Okay, James. Is that all?" She stood closer to him so they were face-to-face now.

He handed her a book. "I want you to have this."

Rose took it from him with care and snuck a peek at the title. *Jane Eyre* by Charlotte Brontë. She would be polite about the gift, but she didn't read classics. That was her sister's preference. Rose liked fantasy books.

"You didn't have to do that." She cradled the book in her arms.

James picked a piece of notebook paper off of his desk and reached around her, sliding it into the front pocket of her backpack. "There. Now you have my phone number." He smiled at her again. "But don't tell anyone about this, okay? We wouldn't want anyone to get the wrong idea."

"Right. I won't tell anyone," Rose promised.

"Okay, then." He leaned in closer to her face with his arm still around her backpack. He let go and patted her arm. "Have a nice Christmas. Text me after you read the book."

"I will."

She hurried off to catch up to Spencer, shoving the book into her backpack. When she got home, she threw her backpack into her closet and forgot all about it until the next semester started.

***

Freshman year – January

Rose strolled through the school hallway with Spencer by her side, as usual. They entered the English classroom, Mr. Mortensen's class, expecting to see his familiar, handsome face. But he wasn't there. Instead, a middle-aged woman with her white-blonde hair in a tight bun stood at the front of the classroom in front of the whiteboard. She greeted everyone as they entered and introduced herself as Mrs. Curton.

Rose wondered if she was the only one wanting an explanation for what had happened to Mr. Mortensen. She contemplated raising her hand to ask, but she didn't want anyone to make assumptions. She had only flirted with him a few times. Okay, and they had made out once in the supply closet, but that was it!

She had thought about him over winter break, and as much as she wanted to kiss him again, she knew it was stupid—not to mention wrong. He was an adult, and she was fifteen. She had planned to end it with him today, so it was a relief knowing she wouldn't have to face him.

He was gone, and she would never have to see him again.

When English ended, Rose followed Spencer out of the classroom toward their lockers. Rose spun the dial and opened her locker.

Spencer leaned in close to her to whisper, "Did you hear the rumors about Mr. Mortensen?"

Rose stiffened beside her best friend. "Um, no. What are people saying?"

This couldn't be about her, could it?

"Everyone says he asked to be transferred to the middle school with no explanation or notice, so I guess he works there now. But a few girls in our grade complained about him making them uncomfortable and flirting with them. Crazy, right?" Spencer said.

"Yeah, crazy. Well, I have to get to my next class. See you later, Spence!" Rose abruptly slammed her locker shut without grabbing her textbooks and speed walked to the other side of the school.

Rose didn't want Spencer to notice her shaking hands. He would want to know what was wrong, and she couldn't tell him. But it was fine. Mr. Mortensen had flirted with girls at the high school, but middle schoolers were off-limits. That was too young even for a creep. She couldn't tell anyone because then she would have to admit what had happened, and that was a secret she didn't want anyone to know.

Chapter 31: Lily

Three weeks ago

A week passed without James letting her leave the guest room. Earlier that day, she had heard the doorbell ring multiple times after James left for work. Was it Holly? How long would it take for her to call the police if Lily didn't answer the door? Holly was the only person besides James who knew where she was. The realization wasn't comforting. She had left her life up to chance and regretted every decision she had made for the past year.

Lily spent all her time coming up with ways to escape, including searching the room for anything she could use as a weapon. While she was searching, the only useful item she found was the bobby pin she had hidden under the mattress in February. She kept it in her enclosed fist, biding her time until James came in with her one meal for the day. If she could stab one of his eyes, he would be temporarily disarmed, and she could run past him to the front door.

When Lily heard the garage door open, her body tensed in preparation. She sat on the bed staring at the door, willing it to open so she could get this over with. She expected to hear James's footsteps coming toward her room, but instead, she heard a second set of footsteps. Someone was visiting again. More people had been over lately. She wasn't sure what that meant for her, but it couldn't be good. She needed to get away before James took her somewhere else . . . or worse.

Lily crept over to the door to listen. She heard the same familiar voice she had heard last week, the voice that had haunted her for seven days because it meant the worst type of betrayal if he was working with James. Her sister's best friend—Spencer.

Chapter 32: Rose

Present day

The rest of June passed in a pile of lazy, hazy summer days. By the time it was July, the heat was at an all-time high in South Carolina. Rose could barely handle being outside for more than a few minutes at a time, so she and Spencer spent most of their time together playing video games, going to Hub City Scoops for ice cream, and swimming at Kasey's house once a week.

Rose hadn't received another note, and after she confronted Mason, she assumed The Midnight Flower was done messing with her—and good riddance to that. She had nearly forgotten all about the harassment, stalking, and threats, until the Fourth of July celebration in downtown Spartanburg.

Spencer had asked her to attend the festival with him. Rose had agreed, even though it was sure to be another sweltering day. They planned to wait until the evening to head downtown. Parking would be a nightmare that late in the day, but they would avoid the worst of the heat.

The sun dipped below the horizon as they strolled out of the parking garage and toward the open field where the fireworks display took place. Spencer had two folding chairs tucked under his arm, while Rose carried a small bag with snacks and drinks. They planned to stay and watch the fireworks for a few hours like most people did.

By the time they found a clear spot to place their chairs with a not-completely-horrible view of the fireworks, they both wearily sat down. Sweat already dripped down her back through her thin tank top. She pulled the tank top free from her skin and fanned her face with her hand.

"It's so gross out," she whined.

Spencer handed her a water bottle. "Stay hydrated. It will help."

Rose groaned but took the water bottle from him anyway. She unscrewed the cap and took a sip of water, not feeling any relief from the already-warming drink, with condensation dripping off the water bottle. She set it on the ground and leaned her head back against the chair, her clothes sticking to her body.

Spencer reached for her hand and held it, swinging their hands together in the air between their chairs. "Thanks for coming with me."

Rose smirked at him and squeezed his hand before letting go. "We go together every year."

"Yeah, but . . . not like this."

"I know what you meant. And you're welcome."

"Don't act like you're doing me some huge favor!" Spencer joked.

"I'm glad I came, even if I melt into a puddle by the time the fireworks are done," Rose teased, swigging more of her water to quench her ever-growing thirst.

"I'll probably be a puddle too, so I guess we'll be puddles together."

"You are *so weird*."

The sun finished its daily duty and set, with the darkness creeping up and stealing the last of the light away until tomorrow. People around them started cheering and clapping in anticipation of the fireworks.

Spencer turned to her with an eager grin on his face. "It's starting soon."

Rose giggled. "I love how excited you are. Just like when we were kids." She settled back into her chair, adjusting her position to get comfortable.

Spencer opened the bag by his feet and hid an item behind his back before she could see it.

"What's that?" she asked curiously.

"A surprise. Guess left or right," he told her, keeping his hands behind his back.

"Uh, right?"

Spencer smiled and held his hands in front of his body, unfurling them to reveal two popsicles.

A crease formed on Rose's forehead. "You know those popsicles are exactly the same, don't you?"

"Yeah, I wanted to see what you would do." He snickered and handed her the one in his right hand.

"Thanks, Spence." She took the popsicle gratefully, peeled off the wrapper, and licked the popsicle before it started melting.

The fireworks show finally began. Rose finished her popsicle and placed her sticky hand on top of Spencer's. They held hands and watched the fireworks. Colors exploded across the sky in a dazzling display. Kids squealed with delight, and even their parents seemed impressed.

Rose felt at peace for the first time in weeks. That should have been the first sign that trouble was brewing.

***

Ripping off another piece of warm, flaky cinnamon roll from the plate in front of her, she swatted Spencer's hand away, shielding the plate protectively with her hand. She almost moved her barstool away from him to emphasize her point. Maybe there was an open spot further down, on the other side of the counter.

"Boyfriend tax?" Spencer said with a hopeful smile.

"I told you to get your own!" Rose reminded him.

"I thought you were kidding . . ." Spencer stared longingly at the cinnamon roll, then glanced at the increasingly long line of people waiting to order that wrapped around the tiny restaurant.

Blue Moon had the best cinnamon rolls in Spartanburg. Rose could easily demolish an entire gigantic cinnamon roll by herself, so she had warned Spencer to order two, but he hadn't listened. She was sure he regretted it as he watched her feasting on her delicious breakfast that was more like a dessert. She giggled as he ate his omelet doused in hot sauce. Sure, the omelet was probably good, but not nearly as delightful as the gooey, fresh cinnamon roll.

Rose stopped eating to pull out her cell phone. "Selfie?" she asked, waving her phone in front of Spencer.

He sighed. "Fine."

Spencer leaned closer to her on his barstool, a cheesy grin on his face as she snapped several photos.

"Thank you." Rose kissed him on the cheek, then swiped up on her phone to check out the pictures.

Her eyes were closed in one of them, but in the second one they were both smiling and looked happy and adorable. She posted the photo on social media and checked into Blue Moon, tagging the location in her post. She captioned the post, *Breakfast date with my fav. Best cinnamon rolls ever!*

Spencer peered over her shoulder to read the post. "Do you have to do that?"

"What?" Rose furrowed her brow and checked out the photo again. "Do you not want people to know we're together?"

He shook his head. "That's not it. I mean posting your entire life on social media."

"Are you really judging me right now?" She ripped off a sizeable chunk of the cinnamon roll and popped it into her mouth, as if in spite. "I was *thinking* about sharing..."

"Some moments, moments like this, are better when they're private. Just between the two of us. If I could, I would scream from a rooftop that you're mine. I really like you, Rose."

Her scrunched-up face relaxed and softened. "I like you too, Spence."

Spencer leaned close to her again, his warm breath on her face. He closed his eyes and tilted his head toward her. Rose tipped her head slightly back and cleared her throat.

"Not in here," she said quietly.

Spencer's face flushed red, and he quickly sat back on the barstool, nearly falling off. He jerked forward to hold on to the rough wooden counter in front of him and managed to keep himself on the stool.

Rose placed a gentle hand on his shoulder. "Later, okay?" she promised, with what she hoped was a flirty smile. But she was awkward and hopeless and could only pray that he didn't think she was inept when it came to dating.

Too late for that.

Spencer had witnessed her floundering with almost every relationship she had ever been in. The only relationship where she had thought it might work out was with Kylar. Their romance hadn't lasted long enough for her to figure herself out, though. She had been young and foolish, so she had ruined it like she ruined everything. But now that she and Spencer were dating, Rose planned to keep him close. Especially because if their relationship ended, it would be catastrophic for so many reasons—one of the most important being that their moms were also best friends, and Spencer lived across the street from her.

After the awkward almost-kiss, Spencer finally spoke. "Are you almost ready to go?"

Rose shoved the plate with the cinnamon roll toward Spencer. Only about a quarter of the delicious treat remained, but it was the least she could do to save him from his embarrassment.

A small smile crawled across Spencer's face. "Oh, so all I needed to do to get part of your cinnamon roll was almost fall to my death and make an ass out of myself? Good to know."

"Yup, file that away for future reference." She tore off one last piece of the cinnamon roll and let him have the rest.

By the time Rose glanced at the plate again, it was empty. Spencer grabbed their dishes and brought them to the dirty dish station, while she picked up her purse that had been sitting on the empty barstool next to her.

"Ready?" Spencer asked.

"Yeah," Rose replied.

But before they could leave the restaurant, someone wearing a black hood and a mask came blasting through the door, nearly knocking Rose over.

"Hey! Watch it!" Spencer warned the stranger.

Rose froze in her tracks, The Midnight Flower blocking her path.

Chapter 33: Lily

Three weeks ago

Lily couldn't hear much of the muffled conversation through the door, but she gathered that Spencer and another man were talking to James. They were planning the big reveal, and Rose was going to be brought here. That didn't sound good for Lily or her sister.

When she heard footsteps, Lily bounced onto the bed and sat down, gazing up at the ceiling.

The doorknob turned, and James entered the room with a tray of food in his hands. He set it on the dresser and sat on the edge of her bed.

"Hello, Lily. Have you thought about what we discussed?" he asked.

"Yes," Lily replied.

"Good. Did you change your mind?"

Lily nodded.

A smile crossed his face. "And what do you think now, Lily?"

Lily crawled toward him on the bed, the bobby pin clutched tightly in her fist.

He smirked in anticipation, as if he thought she was moving toward him for pleasure. But she wasn't. All she had planned for him was pain.

In one swift move, she slashed the bobby pin across his face, but it wasn't sharp enough to leave more than a scratch. She raised it toward his eye, but his hand clamped down on her fist before she could strike him again.

Lily gulped, her heart thundering with fear.

Complete and utter malice crossed James's face as he stared down at her, snatching the bobby pin from her hand. "Lily, I don't think you've learned your lesson yet. I'm a fantastic teacher, so I assume I simply need to switch my methods. I've been more than patient with you." His dark green eyes flashed. "But now I'm going to take what I want, and you're going to let me. No one is here to stop me, and no one cares about what happens to you."

Lily kicked him in the chest and screamed, "You can do whatever you want, but it won't make me love you."

Chapter 34: Rose

Present day

Rose felt only marginally safer with Spencer standing next to her. They were both frozen, waiting for The Midnight Flower to act.

"What do you want, Mason?" Spencer seethed as if reading her mind.

The Midnight Flower shook their head back and forth slowly and held out their open palm with a note.

Spencer glowered at The Midnight Flower, then turned to her. "Don't take the note. Why don't you man up and show your face?" Spencer reached out with his hand moving toward The Midnight Flower's face, as if he was going to take off the mask.

The Midnight Flower took a step back. He spoke in a voice that was deep and husky. He didn't sound like Mason. Was he using one of those voice-changing apps?

"Take the note, Rose. You'll need it if you want your secret to stay between us."

"What secret?" she blurted out, her heart pounding in her chest erratically. Without thinking, she reached out for Spencer's hand for comfort. He responded by squeezing her hand tightly and not letting go.

The Midnight Flower shook his head. "I'm disappointed in you, Rose.

I thought you would have figured out who I am by now. That proves you're as selfish as I thought. I hoped you would change."

By this point, the other people in the small, crowded restaurant were gawking at the spectacle. Rose wanted to leave.

"Let's go," she told Spencer, tugging him back toward the door.

"Okay." But Spencer surprised her by taking the note from The Midnight Flower's still outstretched hand.

"He isn't who you think he is, Rose," The Midnight Flower warned her, pointing at Spencer. "He has a secret of his own."

Just as Rose was going to ask what the hell he was talking about, The Midnight Flower pulled a hidden item out of one of the pockets in their hoodie. With a flick of their wrist, plumes of grayish-black smoke enveloped him. Other patrons in the restaurant began leaving because of the disturbance to their breakfast. The restaurant owner came out and promised everyone the scene was over, then glared at Rose and Spencer accusingly.

The smoke wafted toward them, making Rose cough as she inhaled too much of it. She held her hand over her nose and tried to breathe through it. Spencer wrapped his arms around her, and she burrowed her head into his chest while they waited for the smoke to disappear.

But when the smoke had cleared enough for them to see again, The Midnight Flower was gone.

***

One year ago

Midnight snuck up on them. Spencer alerted her to the time as soon as it was officially the next day.

"We stayed until midnight like you wanted, so can we leave?" Spencer asked with a slight whine to his voice.

Rose groaned and shook the nearly empty bottle of rum. "Fine. We're almost out of alcohol anyway."

Spencer jerked his head toward the bottle. "What are you going to do about that, so your dad doesn't notice you drank it all?"

"It was half empty when I took it. I'll refill it with another liquid and use food coloring to make sure the color matches if I need to." Rose replaced the cap on the bottle and stowed it in her bag.

Spencer stood from his perch on the rock across from her. "Got everything?"

Rose surveyed the surrounding area for anything non-nature related and out of place. She zipped her backpack and pulled it onto her back. "I think I'm good."

"I'll walk you home."

"Because it's *so far* and *so dangerous*," she teased in a lilting voice, shoving him toward the well-worn trail.

Rose matched Spencer's quick pace down the trail, out of the woods, and back into their neighborhood. Her house was directly across the street from his. He followed her to her front door and said goodnight.

"See you tomorrow!" she called after him, turning to face the door and unlocking it.

Almost as soon as she was inside the house, her parents accosted her.

Her mom pulled her close to her chest for a hug, and her dad awkwardly patted her shoulder.

Her mom spoke first, monumental worry and fear—the type that only a mother could possess—coating her voice. She peered around Rose to poke her head outside. "We were so worried about you two when we noticed you both snuck out! Where's Lily?"

Chapter 35: Rose

Present day

When they were safely back at her house, Rose couldn't stop herself from bringing up the truth bomb The Midnight Flower had dropped on her. She needed to know what Spencer was hiding from her—if The Midnight Flower hadn't lied—although that idea had crossed her mind on the ride home too. If it was Mason, he might be trying to break them up. He was probably pissed at Rose for dumping him in public and in front of Spencer. Who knew what lengths he would go to if it meant tearing them apart?

"What did he mean about you having a secret? Are you keeping a secret from me still, after all we've been through?" Rose asked.

Spencer puffed up his cheeks and exhaled loudly. "There's something I have to tell you about the night—"

"You don't have to say it, Spence! I know what happened. Please don't remind me of one of the worst nights of my life," Rose begged him, tears falling from her eyes against her will. She always tried to keep her emotions in check, but when it came to her sister, she never could.

"It's my fault. I know you blame yourself, but I saw Lily that night after you went into your house," Spencer admitted, his face falling.

"You... what?" Rose said in disbelief. "And you're just now telling me *a year later*? Why didn't you tell my parents, or better yet, the police?"

Moving from her spot next to him on the bed, she paced her bedroom. Anxiety filled her to the brim until she was sure she would explode like the fireworks they had seen last night. Except it wouldn't be nearly as pretty.

Spencer sat up straighter, remaining in the same spot on her bed to respect her personal space, and dropped his eyes to his hands in his lap. "I promise I'll tell you, but first, I want you to know that I care about you so much, and I cared about Lily too. I never meant—"

Tears were falling thick and fast, and it was too late for her to stop them. She shook her head, not wanting to believe it. "What did you do, Spence? Tell me."

"When I was crossing the street that night, I saw her riding her bike past your house. I yelled her name, and she stopped riding her bike to look back at me. I swear she made eye contact with me. I told her to go home and talk to you. She was right in front of your house and she looked like she had been crying, so I thought she would go inside. I didn't know what else to do. We didn't have cell phones back then, so I couldn't text you. I was tired and worried about my mom realizing I was gone, so I went inside my house and went to sleep. I thought Lily heard me, but maybe she didn't. After I found out what happened, I kept replaying that night in my head and wondering if that was how it really happened. If I had told someone..." The words tumbled out like Spencer had been holding them in for a long time, waiting to release them. *For an entire year, apparently.*

"Why didn't you tell me?" Rose asked in an accusatory tone.

"Because I didn't want you to hate me. I couldn't stand the thought of losing you. Even back then, I hoped that someday you would see me the way I see you."

"Anything else?" Rose sniffled as she wiped her nose on her hoodie.

"No, that's it."

"How can I ever trust you again?" Rose whispered.

Spencer came over to her, gazing down at her with his hazel eyes watering. He held her hands in his. "Because that's the only secret I've ever kept from you. I've been your best friend since we were babies. I promise I've always, always got your back. There isn't anything I wouldn't do for you, Rose Blackwood."

Rose reflected on the scene at Blue Moon earlier. An icy chill crept over her entire body, despite the sweltering heat. "Spence . . ."

"Hmm?"

"How did The Midnight Flower know you were keeping that from me?"

Spencer wrung his hands together as he stared down at her. "I don't know, Rose. Do you think we were wrong about him being Mason? How could anyone know my worst secret?"

Chapter 36: Rose

Present day

The question circling Rose's mind that night was the true identity of The Midnight Flower. When she had been at Blue Moon earlier and came face-to-face with them, she wished she or Spencer had been brave enough to rip the creepy mask from the mysterious person's face. But neither of them had done it, as they were too distracted by causing a scene in the small, crowded restaurant and escaping safely.

When Rose thought about it more, she resolved herself to uncover the truth. After Spencer had told her the reality about what happened one year ago after he brought her home, she couldn't get it out of her head. Part of her wished she had known sooner, but she wasn't sure if that would have changed the outcome. Probably not, considering the police had never found Lily's body.

***

One year ago

"Is Lily outside still?" Her mom opened the front door and scanned the driveway. She turned back to Rose, her face conveying the depth of her fear. She gripped Rose by the shoulders and shook her. "Where is Lily? She's with you, isn't she?" she asked frantically.

Rose pried her mom's fingers from her arms. Her dad pulled her mom back and stared at her too, only doing marginally better at not collapsing into full-blown panic.

"Where's your sister, Rose?" her dad asked in a stern tone.

"How should I know? I was out with Spencer." Rose shrugged her shoulders, wondering what the big deal was.

"If you're lying for her, this isn't a game. Tell us where she is, so we can all go to bed," her dad said, glowering at her.

"I—I'm not lying, Dad, I swear. I thought she was at home. I haven't seen her tonight." The lie came out milliseconds before Rose comprehended the gravity of the situation.

A sob escaped from her mom, and she collapsed against her dad. He put his arms around her and soothed her.

"I'm calling 911," her dad said, springing into action. "You two should go wait in the family room. We have to talk to the police. The sooner we find her, the better."

Rose led her mom over to the black leather couch in the family room and sat next to her, holding her hand while her dad called the police. A fuzzy feeling came over her, as if she was dreaming. Or maybe she was drunk from all the rum.

She had seen Lily less than two hours ago. She couldn't be missing. Her sister couldn't be gone.

***

Present day

Rose was cleaning out her bag when she found the note from The Midnight Flower that he had given her yesterday at Blue Moon. She read it carefully, her eyes welling up with tears.

Rose,
Do you ever wonder what happened to your sister? Don't you know what happened that night, one year ago, when you told her to walk home alone? Do you want to know her fate? I bet your parents still blame you for not watching her. You're her older sister. You should have protected Lily. Are you scared your sister is dead, and it's all your fault?
The Midnight Flower

Sobbing, Rose placed the newest note with the others and locked them in her desk drawer in her bedroom, making sure they were safely hidden. She didn't want her parents to know what was going on. They had been so paranoid since her sister's disappearance and had done their best to protect Rose. If they thought she was in danger, they would never let her leave the house again. Losing one daughter was bad enough. If they lost Rose too, who knew what would happen to them? Rose feared they wouldn't survive, so she had to keep the notes and the stalking to herself for her parents' sakes. She had to solve the mystery of The Midnight Flower on her own.

Chapter 37: Rose

Present day

While scrolling through social media, Rose received a new notification.

Holly Gray liked one of your photos.

Taken aback, Rose clicked on the notification to see the photo. It was a selfie she had taken last summer when she was at the beach with Holly, an angled shot of her body in a bikini. Chills crept over her skin, and she contemplated deleting the photo.

Without thinking much about it, she messaged Holly on the app.

Rose: Hey, how are you?

Immediately, she received a new notification. *Holly Gray has blocked you.*

What the heck? Rose attempted clicking on Holly's profile, but she couldn't. The profile was grayed out as if it no longer existed. Why had Holly been creeping on her profile, liking old photos, and then blocked her as soon as Rose reached out to her? For a few seconds, Rose thought Holly wanted to resolve things. Maybe she wanted to put the past behind them and move on for good. Rose would have been all for that idea. Clearly, that wasn't the case.

Rose continued scrolling through her social media apps for ten more minutes until she became bored. Her mind drifted to Mason and how their relationship had gone horribly wrong. There was a small part of her that didn't believe he was The Midnight Flower. She reminded herself that he hadn't treated her with respect and didn't care about her. He had been weirdly obsessed with Lily, but did he hate her enough to scare her and blackmail her?

Besides, she still didn't know how The Midnight Flower knew so much about her and Spencer, not to mention Lily's disappearance. Either they had a way of watching them or listening in on their conversations, or someone else they knew was involved.

For the first time, the scariest thought of all crossed Rose's mind.

What if Spencer is The Midnight Flower?

Almost as soon as she considered it, she chuckled darkly and shut the idea down. It wasn't possible. She and Spencer had known each other their entire lives, and their moms were best friends too. They had grown up on the same street. They had gone through childhood together, awkward years and all. That sort of friendship didn't end in betrayal without a truly awful event instigating it, and what had she ever done to Spencer that would result in him betraying her? Nothing she could think of.

Rose needed to talk to Mason and Spencer to piece together more of the puzzle. If she wanted to solve the mystery and evade the clutches of The Midnight Flower, she needed to interrogate everyone who could be involved, including her evil exes.

***

Rose told her parents where she was going, just in case. As usual, they were wary about her going anywhere, but she told them she would be in a public place with plenty of witnesses.

She met Mason at the same coffee shop she frequented with Spencer.

Spill the Beans was downtown, so she drove there in only a few minutes.

She was sitting on one of the cozy armchairs by the fireplace—which wasn't emitting any heat because it was another ninety-degree day in July. On the rectangular oak table in front of her, a mostly empty plastic cup with a little iced coffee and a lot of ice remained. Mason was late, and she wasn't sure he would show up. After their dramatic break-up, she doubted he wanted to see her. And to be honest, she didn't want to see him again either, but it was necessary if she wanted to stop The Midnight Flower.

Rose pulled out her phone, debating if she should text Mason to ask where he was when he strode through the door and sat down next to her.

"Hi, Mason," she greeted him, remaining seated.

"Hi." He stood next to her chair.

"Thanks for meeting me. I know this is awkward, but I need to talk to you," she started, struggling to remember what she had rehearsed in the car on the way over.

Mason peered down at her, his blue eyes sparkling dangerously. "Is this about The Midnight Flower?"

Rose swallowed, resisting the urge to scream or run out of the coffee shop. Now, more than ever, she knew she had to do this. "How did you know?"

"Because they contacted me too," he said.

"What?" Rose stared at him, uncomprehending. She hadn't expected that. "What do they want from you?"

"I'm assuming the same thing they want from you. For my secret to be revealed. I refused, and they backed off for a while, but they started harassing me again this week. I thought I was safe, but I don't know how far they're willing to take it. Be careful, Rose. They're dangerous," Mason warned her.

"Do you know who they are?"

"No. Every time we've met up, they're always wearing a black hoodie and this weird mask covering their face. They use a voice-changing app when they talk, so I can't tell who they are. Do you have any ideas?" Mason sat in the oversized armchair next to her, rested his elbow on the armrest of the chair, and leaned toward her.

Rose wouldn't reveal any details to Mason that she didn't need to, so she shook her head.

Mason sighed in disappointment. "I was hoping you had more information than I did and that we could figure this out together."

"Sorry, I, uh . . ." Rose stumbled over her words, embarrassed about why she had asked to meet with Mason.

He tilted his head to the side. "What?"

"I thought you might be The Midnight Flower," she admitted.

Mason chuckled and rubbed the stubble on his chin. "No, it's not me. But if I was The Midnight Flower, I wouldn't tell you, anyway." He winked. "Be careful who you trust, Rose."

***

"Rose, why the hell didn't you call me? I would have gone with you. Do you have any idea how dangerous that was? Mason could have hurt you!" Spencer exploded.

Rose held her cell phone away from her ear as he continued ranting. She sat in front of her desk in her bedroom, staring at the photo collage on the wall across from her. Photos of her and Spencer throughout the years, and one of her and Lily that she hadn't taken down, were scattered across the wall, although it pained her every time she spotted Lily's bright, young face. She turned away from the photo of her sister.

"I know, I know. I don't need a lecture from you about it. But Mason isn't The Midnight Flower, and I'm fine. He wouldn't have agreed to meet me if you were there. He was civil the entire time," she promised.

"Yeah, because you were in a public space, and he doesn't want you to suspect him. We might have questioned if it was him, but we don't know for sure that he isn't involved. We need to narrow it down and find out their identity."

"It's not that simple. The Midnight Flower won't admit who they are or what they're doing. They clearly enjoy holding people's secrets over them and feeling powerful and in control. We need to force them out of hiding and make them show themselves. We need to stop giving them a choice and keeping us in fear. It's time to unmask them," Rose explained.

"Do you have an idea?" Spencer asked, sounding wary.

"Yup, but I'm going to need your help."

"Ugh, I was afraid you were going to say that. Okay, I'm in, but only because I don't want you doing this on your own. I don't want something to happen to you."

Rose grinned. Spencer was her best friend for a reason. "Good. So, here's what we need to do first . . ."

Chapter 38: Rose

Present day

Scuttling through the trees, Rose came out into the clearing. She didn't want to relive that night, but she didn't have a choice if she wanted to stop The Midnight Flower. This was the only way to find out what had happened to her sister. Spencer stood on guard next to her, watching her cautiously as she retraced their steps and summarized what had happened one year ago. They moved through their actions as well as they could remember, then went back to her house afterward to recap.

"And after you saw Lily riding her bike . . . nothing else happened?" Rose prompted, tapping a pen against her notebook.

"That was the last time I saw your sister," Spencer answered.

"Okay. It's impossible to know where she went after that. Whether she rode her bike around the neighborhood or went somewhere else . . . I can't imagine her leaving our neighborhood so late at night, especially by herself. Our parents didn't let us go out that late."

"Yeah, but you clearly broke that rule too," Spencer said pointedly.

"I know. But I don't think Lily would have snuck out if I hadn't done it first. She only came out that night because she wanted to hang out with us."

"Didn't the police go over all of this when your parents reported her as missing last year?" Spencer asked.

"Yeah, but they could have missed something. The police aren't perfect. They never found her." Rose chewed on her lip.

"Well, yeah, but she's been gone for almost a year, Rose. Do you really think she's still out there somewhere?"

Tears formed in her eyes. She blinked slowly, trying to prevent herself from collapsing. "Spence, please . . ."

"I'm sorry. I didn't mean to . . . Sorry." He stumbled lamely over his words, then wrapped his arms around her, holding her against his chest and comforting her the best way he knew how.

Taking a deep, shuddering breath, Rose continued, "The anniversary of the day she went missing is next week. I want to have a memorial for everyone to remember her and celebrate her life. I think it will be good for my parents too. They never talk about her, even when I mention her name. They act like she never existed, but she did. I miss her and want to honor her life."

"That's a great idea, Rose. Let me know how I can help. I'll do whatever you need."

"Thanks." She sniffled. "Maybe we can rent out the cultural center downtown. That would be the perfect event space for this."

"I'll do some research. I can ask my mom for help too. She still volunteers at the cultural center sometimes," Spencer offered.

Rose turned to Spencer and buried her head in his chest, wanting to disappear. Sometimes she thought about how different her life would be if Lily was still here, if she still had a sister. If she didn't have overprotective, ultra-paranoid parents who watched her every move. Her life would be normal.

Other times, she couldn't make herself believe Lily was gone, and she pretended her younger sister was out there in the world somewhere. She could have run away and started over somewhere new. But Rose knew that was unlikely. Where would Lily have gone and why would she run away? Lily had only been twelve when she went missing, and the police never found any trace of her. It was as if she had vanished.

***

The day of the memorial had arrived. Rose's parents struggled to talk about Lily, so Rose didn't push them too much. They had agreed to pay for the memorial and to show up shortly before the event started. It would be weird if her own parents weren't there.

Spencer had volunteered to help. He was by her side every day, helping her pick out photos to use for the remembrance video, giving her notes on her speech, and recommending snacks and drinks for everyone who attended. She had never been more thankful for her best friend than she was during that week.

Smoothing out her silky, black skirt, Rose checked herself out in the large rectangular mirror in the bathroom she used to share with Lily. Her black, lacy, short-sleeved blouse was immaculate, but she straightened it out, anyway. She ran a hand through her wavy, red hair and touched up her makeup, which she rarely wore, but today seemed like a good enough occasion to pull out all the stops.

As Rose debated if she should chance wearing high heels or wear her flat silver sandals, the doorbell rang.

A moment later, her mom called from downstairs, "Rose, Spencer's here!"

"Coming!" she yelled back.

Rose slipped on the silver sandals, then threw her keys, wallet, and a few other items into her purse and went downstairs. Her mouth nearly dropped open when she laid her eyes on Spencer. On a daily basis, he was adorable, but this was an entirely different level of hotness. His curly, light brown hair was shiny and freshly combed. He wore a dark gray dress shirt with black slacks and dress shoes.

When their eyes met, he smiled at her in awe, and she knew he felt the same.

"You look beautiful, Rose," he whispered in a voice so sexy she felt her face flushing while her mom stood by the doorway watching them.

"Thanks, you too," she responded, tucking her hair behind her ear.

"You look very handsome, Spencer," her mom said with a smile.

"Mom, we're going there early to set up." Her mom's smile became strained. "See you later?" Rose said.

"Yes, sweetie, we'll be there," her mom choked out. She took off down the hallway toward her bedroom, and the door slammed soon after.

Rose's gaze dropped to the floor. Tears sprang to her eyes. She didn't try to stop them from falling. It was a tough day, and her sister was gone. She didn't need to keep her emotions in check. It was okay if she cried.

Spencer came over to her and tipped her chin up so her green eyes met his hazel eyes.

"I'm here for you. Always," he promised.

"I know. Thank you. I don't know what I would do without you." She wrapped her arms around him, falling into his familiar embrace.

"Luckily, you won't have to find out. I'm yours for as long as you want me." He winked.

"I don't think I'll change my mind anytime soon," she said cheekily, trying to lighten the subject.

"Ah, how romantic. You're making me swoon, Ms. Blackwood," Spencer joked, rubbing her back with one hand while he held her other hand in his.

Rose smiled and shook her head. "Should we get going?"

"Sure. Where's the stuff we need to bring? I'll load up my car."

Rose pointed to the family room. "There are some boxes in there."

Spencer jogged over to the boxes, with Rose following him. Rose handed him the heaviest box and picked up a lighter one, full of photos.

With a grunt, Spencer carried the box to his car, loaded it into the trunk, then took the box Rose was holding from her arms.

When they had finished loading the car, Spencer opened the passenger door and Rose got inside the car. They arrived downtown. Spencer struggled to find a parking spot and had to circle the nearby streets multiple times before he had no choice but to go in a parking garage. All the parking lots close to the cultural center were full. There was a festival going on downtown, so the streets were packed.

Together, they brought the boxes into the cultural center and started setting up for the memorial. Rose couldn't believe her parents weren't there with her. She hoped they didn't back out at the last minute. It felt wrong that they weren't at the one-year anniversary memorial of their missing daughter. Didn't they care about Lily? Didn't they want to remember her?

Fuming, Rose accidentally ripped a white streamer in half as her anger got the best of her.

"You okay?" Spencer questioned, moving closer to her. He had been across the room, hanging the rest of the streamers throughout the lobby.

Rose held the broken streamer in her hands and let it fall to the ground and curl against the dark hardwood flooring. A sob escaped from her mouth like a creature waiting to be unleashed from captivity. Wordlessly, Spencer pulled her into his arms and tucked her head against his chest, running one hand through her hair and whispering soothing words to her. Rose didn't know how long they stayed like that—her crying and Spencer comforting her—until she heard someone clear their throat, and she broke away from Spencer.

Kasey waved hello to them awkwardly. "Are you two together?" she asked with an impish grin.

"Oh, uh—" Rose started.

At the same time, Spencer said, "Yes."

Kasey laughed. "Okay, then. Good for you guys. I always wondered why you weren't dating. You're cute together. No one else is here yet? Do you need help setting up?"

Rose wiped her cheeks and groaned. "I bet my makeup is ruined. Do I look like a mess?"

"Of course not," Spencer said, ever the wonderful boyfriend.

"You can go to the bathroom to touch up your makeup. I'll help Spencer with whatever is left," Kasey offered.

"Thank you." Rose snagged her purse from the table where she had left it and headed to the bathroom.

Staring at her reflection in the mirror, she swiped away the clumps of mascara underneath her eyes and re-applied her makeup. When she put the makeup back in her purse, she found an item that hadn't been in there before: a new note from The Midnight Flower.

Her arm hairs stood on end as she wildly searched the bathroom for a sign that someone had been inside, but no one else was in there.

When had The Midnight Flower put the new note in her bag?

Chapter 39: Rose

Sprinting out of the bathroom and practically tripping over her own feet—although she had chosen the more sensible flat sandals—Rose hurried to find Spencer. She entered the grand hall, the entryway with high ceilings and a chandelier sparkling in the center. That was where she had left Spencer and Kasey, so where were they?

"Spence?" she shouted, not spotting him.

Rose kept walking, moving toward the entrance into the auditorium where all the seating and the stage were. "Spence?"

The doors to the auditorium slammed shut. Rose stared at the door she was closest to. Her heart pounded rapidly in her chest, and she contemplated yelling Spencer's name again. What if he wasn't nearby? Where did he go?

It had to be The Midnight Flower. But how had they closed both doors at once? The doors were on opposite sides of the room, so it wasn't humanly possible to do it without help. Not for the first time, the possibility of The Midnight Flower having a partner crossed Rose's mind. It would explain so much if two people were working together. But the question remained: who was it?

Rose tiptoed to the door and pressed her ear against it. She strained to hear any sound that would give away who was inside the auditorium. Backing away from the door, she pulled her bag from her shoulder and slid out the newest note.

Rose,

How sweet of you to host a memorial for Lily! You're almost acting like a real sister would. It doesn't quite make up for her disappearance, but you're trying, and that's what matters, right?

Cancel the memorial now, and make sure everyone leaves, or suffer the consequences. By now, you have to realize that I know all your secrets. How isn't important, but I will destroy you, secret by secret, until you have nothing left.

Yours sincerely,
The Midnight Flower

Stifling a sob, Rose folded the note and tucked it carefully into the inner pocket of her purse. She didn't want to be alone. She needed to find Spencer and Kasey. She questioned if she should listen to them, cancel the memorial, and go home—where she would be relatively safe—but then she reminded herself why she was having the memorial. It was all for Lily. Her sister deserved this remembrance of her too brief life, but she deserved so much more. She couldn't cancel the event because of a stupid note.

She entered the auditorium, where Spencer and Kasey were embracing.

"Spencer, I was looking for you," Rose spoke up. "Did you see who shut the doors?"

"What?" Kasey asked. Her soft smile turned to confusion.

Spencer stepped away from Kasey. "Rose! Kasey told me her good news."

Rose turned to Kasey expectantly. "What's up?"

Kasey waved around a piece of paper with excitement clearly etched across her pale face. "I got into Clemson! Early acceptance!"

"Wow! Already? We're only going to be juniors in the fall," Rose said.

Kasey's head bobbed up and down. "Yeah! I've been taking college classes, and I guess they decided I was qualified."

Spencer bumped her shoulder with his. "Clearly, you're more than qualified. You're brilliant. Congrats again." He moved toward Rose and planted a loud kiss on her cheek. "You okay?" he asked, noticing the withdrawn, worried expression on her face.

"Mmhmm," she muttered, barely able to speak because her mind was running a hundred miles per hour.

"What were you saying about the doors?" Kasey asked.

Spencer shrugged his shoulders. "They shut just before I came in here. I propped them open, but I guess it didn't work."

Rose couldn't help but feel suspicious. Spencer's explanation sounded lame. Were they lying to her about why they were in here? Could they both be The Midnight Flower? They had been alone in the auditorium this whole time. One of them could have planted the note in her bag when they first arrived here. They could have shut the doors together to scare her.

But Spencer wouldn't do that to her, right? And Kasey had always been a good friend, never giving Rose a reason to distrust her. In fact, some of their classmates at school had bullied Kasey, so if anyone understood what it was like to have a tormentor, it was Kasey. She couldn't be responsible for this.

"Hello-o-o?" A husky voice came from outside the auditorium.

"People are showing up. Should we go greet them, or do you need a minute? I can go out there if you want to stay in here and collect yourself first." Spencer pointed to the door.

"Uh, no, I'm okay. We can go." Rose started toward the door. "Come in! We're in the auditorium," she replied to the mysterious person, barely noticing the deep, husky voice that should have been familiar.

As Rose approached the door, the lights in the auditorium went out, thrusting the three of them into darkness.

Blindly, Rose reached out for the door. She knew it was close. She could find it if she felt around for it. It should have been only a few feet away.

"Spence, where are you?" she said in a low voice.

"Over here," he said, sounding further away than he had been a moment ago.

"Can you find the door? Wait a sec. I have my cell phone in my purse." Rose dug around inside her purse and found her phone, flicking on the flashlight app.

Seconds later, two other lights sparked in the darkened room. Rose sighed with relief. Spencer and Kasey must have found their phones too. They would be fine. They could use their cell phone flashlights to find the door and get out of there.

A fourth light popped up, casting its light toward Rose, coming toward her at an alarming rate.

Someone else was in the room with them.

Chapter 40: Rose

Rose woke up feeling groggy and disoriented. She rubbed her aching head and slowly sat up from her position on the ground. Why was she lying on the ground? Her head throbbed painfully, and the room was too dark to see much. She cast her gaze around, waiting for her eyes to adjust to the lack of light. Brushing her hands across the floor, she searched for her cell phone. She needed a light. She must have dropped her phone when—

Wait a second. The last thing Rose remembered was the lights going out. But what had happened after that? Spencer and Kasey had been with her, so where were they?

"Spence! Kasey!" she yelled, straining her eyes in the darkness. It wasn't pitch black, but it was difficult to make out much more than vague shapes.

If her friends weren't with her, what had happened to them? Panic and adrenaline fluttered in her stomach like the feeling of going down an incredibly high drop on a rollercoaster. She scrambled to her feet and groaned, rubbing the back of her head again. She winced as she touched the sore spot and removed her hand. *Is that blood?*

Rose put her arms out in front of her and cautiously inched forward.

Before she passed out, she had been close to one of the doors. If she walked forward a few steps, then she should be able to get out. However, after three steps forward, her arms didn't reach the door. Instead, she felt metal. When she reached lower, she felt rows of shelves. There weren't shelves in the auditorium. *Where am I?*

"Spencer? Kasey?" she shouted, louder this time.

Rose circled the room, discovering it was only a few feet wide on each side. She found a broom, a mop, and cleaning supplies. She wasn't in the auditorium anymore; that much was obvious. But why was she in a supply closet? Had someone knocked her unconscious and put her in here? What was The Midnight Flower's plan? Thoughts of what they wanted with her entered her mind, sending her fear skyrocketing through the roof.

Sinking back down onto the cool linoleum floor, she held her head in her hands as she sobbed. She needed to find her inner strength and figure out how to get out of the closet, but she couldn't do that yet. She needed a moment to wallow. This day wasn't going at all how she had planned.

After allowing herself to cry for a few minutes, Rose stood up and felt around the closet, searching for a light switch. She found the light switch and flicked it up. A dim, yellowish light emitted from a single chain bulb on the ceiling.

Squinting, she let her eyes adjust to the light. She reached out for the doorknob, but to her immense dismay, it turned only part of the way, like it was jammed. Or something outside the closet was holding the doorknob shut.

Great.

Now she needed to find a tool to open the door.

As she dug through the shelves, she heard footsteps outside the closet.

"Hello? Is someone out there? Please help! I'm in the closet. I'm locked in here."

The doorknob rattled. Rose stepped back from the door. Who was out there? Why weren't they answering?

She moved back further until her back pressed against the far wall. She grabbed a hammer from the shelf. Clutching it in her right hand, she prepared to strike someone down.

The doorknob opened. Spencer's curly, brown head popped into view. "Rose?"

With a clang, the hammer fell from her hands and onto the floor. "Spencer!" she screeched, launching herself into his arms, wanting to feel safe.

"What were you doing in there? And what were you planning to do with that hammer?" He surveyed the closet and kept an arm around her as if he sensed her fear and anxiety.

"I don't know how I ended up in there. After the lights went out in the auditorium, someone hit me on the back of my head. I woke up in here." Rose clung to his shirt, gripping the silky fabric in her hands and not wanting him to leave her side ever again.

"Oh my God, Rose. Your head is bleeding! We need to get you to the emergency room!" Spencer gently touched the back of her head. His hand came away with blood on it. He stared at his bloody hand. "Who did this to you?"

Rose shook her head, tears threatening to fall again. "I don't know." Her heart sank. "What about the memorial?"

"Oh. Um . . ." Spencer moved toward a roll of paper towels on the shelf and wiped off his hand.

"What is it? Tell me," Rose demanded.

"Not many people showed up," Spencer admitted, barely able to meet her eyes.

Rose frowned. "Where's Kasey? We need to tell her we're leaving."

Spencer's eyebrows rose. "I'm not sure. I thought maybe you two were together."

Rose gestured around the closet. "She's clearly not in here."

"Then where is she?"

Spencer pulled her away from the closet and shut the door.

Rose glared at him. "Where the hell is Kasey?"

"I don't know. Should we check the auditorium? That's where we were when we got separated."

As much as Rose didn't want to believe it, something terrible could have happened to Kasey. They weren't safe, but she couldn't leave her friend there, alone and defenseless.

"Please call the police, Spence. I don't have my phone, and I don't know where my purse is."

Spencer nodded and did as she asked. After he hung up the phone, Rose inspected his head, then searched for any visible injuries on his body. He appeared fine.

"Hold on. If someone knocked me out and shoved me into a janitor's closet, where were you? Did someone knock you out too?"

"No. When the lights went out, I used my cell phone flashlight and made my way over to the door. By the time I got there, you were gone, which sent me into a panic. After I left the auditorium, I searched most of the cultural center. I was about to call the police when I heard you yelling in here." Spencer bit his lip, and his eyes dropped to the ground. "Honestly, I didn't think about what happened to Kasey. I was so worried about finding you."

"Okay. I'm not sure going back in there is a good idea, though. The police are on their way, right? Maybe we should wait outside," Rose suggested.

"Yeah. They can handle this better than we can. I didn't realize how huge this place was before. Kasey might have left the auditorium and went into another room looking for us. Let's go to the hospital and get your head checked out."

Spencer was right. Her head hadn't stopped throbbing since she woke up. She would feel better when she had some painkillers and confirmation that she was okay. The police would help them find their friend, and Kasey would be fine.

Chapter 41: Rose

Half an hour later, Rose was lying in a hospital bed being examined by a doctor. Thankfully, her head injury wasn't serious, but she needed a few stitches to close up the wound. The doctor prescribed painkillers and told her to rest. Spencer waited in a chair by her bed, promising he wouldn't leave. By the time Rose was dozing off in the stiff hospital bed, her parents came barreling into her room.

"Oh my God, Rose! Are you okay? What happened?" her mom rapid-fired questions, coming up to her bed and clasping Rose's hands in between hers.

Wearily, Rose opened her eyes to face her parents. She explained what had happened, and Spencer chimed in when he had something to add.

"We're so glad you're both okay," her dad said, gripping her shoulder tightly for a few seconds in his only show of comfort. "Is this related to the incident at the house last month?"

"It might be," Rose stated, not wanting to give up all of her secrets yet.

"How was the memorial? We feel awful that we weren't there. It seemed too difficult to go through, but now I wish we had been there with you," her mom said.

Rose sniffled. "Not many people showed up, so you didn't miss much.

I was knocked unconscious before it officially started. I guess it's good that there weren't more people there."

"Yes, especially if whoever did this to you wasn't working alone. Did you tell the police about the other incident?" her dad replied.

She paused, licking her dry, cracked lips. "Um, no."

"I'll handle it, Rose," her dad promised. "Just rest."

"Thanks, Dad. Have you heard an update about Kasey? Is she okay? Spence and I thought she might have gone into a different room at the cultural center. Did the police find her?"

Rose's dad squeezed her mom's hand, and her mom sobbed hysterically.

"What is it? What's wrong?" Rose asked, imagining the worst.

Fear laced throughout Rose at her parents' reactions. Her hands shook as she tried to distract herself by picking up the half-empty glass of water from her bedside table, suddenly unbearably parched. She raised the glass to her lips while her parents stayed silent.

"Please tell me," Rose whispered, her voice scratchy. With trembling hands, she set the glass back on the table.

Her dad took a deep breath, and his face set into a grim expression. "We're really sorry to have to tell you this, Rose, but the police officers called to the scene told us some horrific news. After they searched the rest of the cultural center, they found Kasey, but she's . . . she's dead."

Chapter 42: Rose

"But . . . how? What happened to her?" Rose stared at Spencer to see how he reacted to the awful news, then returned her gaze to her parents.

She crumpled up the thin hospital blanket in her hands, pulling it back from where it was covering her. She wanted to jump out of bed, but she was so dizzy she didn't think she could stand. It had to be from the head trauma and the pain meds. Or the shock of finding out one of her friends was—

Kasey couldn't be dead. *This can't be possible.* It had to be a sick, sick joke. Who would want to kill her? Kasey had never hurt anyone. She was the nerdy, awkward, super sweet, rich girl that Rose and Spencer had befriended during their freshman year because she couldn't make any friends. Or the friends she made only wanted to hang out with her for her pool and her parents' money. Rose and Spencer had welcomed her as genuine friends and valued the time they spent together.

But she was gone.

Ripped from the world much too soon.

She was only sixteen, for God's sake.

Spencer spoke up first, coming closer to Rose and kneeling beside her bed. "She was hanging from the chandelier in the lobby of the cultural center."

Rose's hand flew to her mouth. She felt her meager lunch from much earlier in the day coming up her throat. Her mom handed her the small trash can by her bedside, and her stomach lurched as she leaned over it. Her mom rubbed her back as she threw up.

Afterward, she felt better. Or her stomach did, at least. Rose was so shocked she couldn't even cry. She had already endured more loss from horrific accidents than some people went through in their entire lives. But were they really accidents? Her sister was still technically missing, even a year later, and the police had never solved the case.

Rose knew everyone assumed Lily was dead.

There was no way she hadn't been taken, kidnapped, held hostage, sold into human trafficking, or murdered. Rose never let herself think about her sister's certain demise, but at the news of Kasey's death, all the terrible scenarios she had avoided thinking about flashed through her mind at once, bombarding her with images that shocked her to her core. She was overcome with grief and, more importantly, anger.

This had to be The Midnight Flower. First, her sister. Now her friend ... She would see to it personally that the anonymous killer paid for their crimes.

***

The hospital staff insisted that Rose stay the night in the hospital for observation and to ensure that her head injury hadn't caused permanent brain damage. Her parents had agreed, with her mom demanding they let her sleep in Rose's room with her. Her mom was lightly snoring on a rollaway cot that a nurse had brought in for her earlier.

Rose couldn't sleep, despite the painkillers. She hadn't wanted sleeping pills. She couldn't sleep at a time like this. Sleep was a waste of time, precious time she needed to find The Midnight Flower and stop them, once and for all. Who knew what else they would do if they went unchecked? Whom else would they hurt? Her parents or Spencer . . . She couldn't bear to lose anyone else.

At 3:15 a.m., Rose turned on the TV, deciding she might as well watch trashy reality TV. Finally, she dozed off with one of those shows about housewives on in the background, lulling her into a semi-conscious state.

A creaking sound startled her. Rose rubbed her eyes. A shadowy figure stalked into her hospital room. The mysterious person wore a black hoodie and a mask. The Midnight Flower had come for her. To finish her off. They crept up to her bed, closer and closer until they were mere feet from her bedside.

Rose cowered back, lifting the blanket to her chin. Her eyes watered fiercely.

"Rose . . ." the familiar, deep, husky voice taunted. "Don't you want to know who I am, Rose?" They leaned down toward her face, gesturing to the mask. "Take it off and find out the truth."

As she reached up to pull off the mask, The Midnight Flower snapped their fingers, and a cloud of grayish-black smoke appeared. Just like before at Blue Moon, when the smoke cleared enough to see, they were gone. Vanished like they were never in her room.

Rose started coughing as the smoke crept throughout the room. She stretched out her hand for the glass of water on the table nearby and drank the rest of it. Sighing, she lay back in bed and tried to get comfortable again.

Her mom was on the cot next to her, still sleeping somehow. Rose tried to convince herself that nothing could happen to her. No one could hurt her. She was safe.

Had she imagined The Midnight Flower appearing in her room? How would they have gotten in? And better yet, how did they keep disappearing? Was it magic or witchcraft?

Rose shivered and pulled the blanket closer around her body, tucking herself in with the illusion of safety.

***

Rose heard hushed voices in the hall and forced her eyes to open.

"Ugh," she groaned as her head throbbed. The painkillers must have worn off. Her gaze traveled around the room, but no one else was there.

Her mom must have moved out to the hallway to talk to a doctor. The hushed voices grew silent, then someone knocked on the door.

"Yeah, come in," Rose said.

Her mom entered the room with Spencer. Spencer was holding a tan cardboard box with a duck logo on it from her favorite donut place, as well as a to-go tray full of coffee balanced on top.

Rose beamed when Spencer set the donut box on her bed. Then, with a magnanimous gesture, he told her to open the box and choose whichever one she wanted.

"*One*?" she scoffed, scanning the donuts. "I think I deserve a lot more than one measly donut."

Spencer chuckled. "You're right. Eat as many as you want."

He sat next to her while she selected one with Oreo crumbles, marshmallow drizzle, and crushed graham crackers.

"Mmm," she said through a mouthful of donut. "Thanks, Spence. You really know how to treat a girl."

Her mom laughed, shaking her head at their antics. "The doctor said you'll be discharged today. I could really use a shower and some clean clothes, but I don't want to leave you."

"It's okay, Mom. Spence will bring me home, right?" Rose replied.

Spencer nodded as he gazed longingly at the donuts. "That's fine with me. I don't mind. As long as you share a donut."

Rose's mom gathered up her belongings and folded her coat over her arm. "Well, I don't know . . . Should I really be leaving you here alone right now?"

"I won't be alone, though. Spence will be—" Rose started.

"I won't leave her side, Celia. I promise," Spencer said.

Rose's mom nodded. "Please make sure she gets home safely, Spencer."

"Of course," he said.

"I love you, sweetie." Her mom bent down to embrace her.

"Love you too, Mom," she mumbled through a mouthful of donut.

Her mom raised an eyebrow at her.

"Sorry." Rose cleared her throat, swallowing the rest of the donut.

Her mom left the room and shut the door. A forced grin spread across Spencer's face, but he was otherwise pale and withdrawn, with bags under his eyes.

"Are you okay?" she asked, peering at him intently. She caressed his cheek with her hand and closed the donut box, setting it on the rolling bedside table.

Spencer had been reaching for the donut box, so he protested, "I'm fine. Hey! Why did you move those away from me?"

"Did you sleep last night?" Rose questioned. She wasn't hungry anymore.

"Nope. What about you?"

"No. I kept thinking about Kasey. And . . . and Lily." Rose rested her head on Spencer's shoulder. "Spence, I have to tell you something. I think someone was here last night."

Spencer sat up straighter and became more alert. "What? What happened now? Did someone hurt you again?"

Rose shook her head. "The Midnight Flower visited me."

Chapter 43: Rose

"What?" Spencer spat, his eyes turning to venom. "The Midnight Flower was here last night?" His eyes darted nervously around the tiny hospital room as if he was searching for proof.

"Yeah, they snuck in here in the middle of the night. They asked if I wanted to know who they were. Then they told me to take off their mask and find out the truth."

"Are you sure you weren't dreaming? Did your mom see him?" Spencer asked warily.

"I don't think so. I didn't tell her. She doesn't need me to add to her stress. I'm sure my mom is worried enough about me already." Rose broke eye contact with Spencer, not wanting to meet his eyes at this revelation.

"If The Midnight Flower was really here, and they were at your house before too, then I don't think you're safe anywhere. Now that your parents know someone is stalking you, they'll want to keep you safe. We can ask your dad to install security cameras outside your house to monitor anyone who comes by. Then we can—"

"Whoa, Spencer, it's okay. I'll be fine," Rose promised, although her stomach twisted. She didn't want Spencer or her parents to worry about her even more.

Spencer picked up her hand and brought it to his lips, planting a kiss on it. "I promise I'll keep you safe. I won't let anything happen to you, no matter what."

Overcome with exhaustion, Rose didn't respond; instead, she slipped back into a dreamless sleep with Spencer by her side.

***

When Rose woke up, Spencer handed her a fresh coffee. "Here."

She sipped it slowly, savoring the warmth and jolt of caffeine through her exhausted body. "Thanks."

"By the way, while you slept, I went to talk to the nurse and the security guard on duty. The security guard checked the cameras, Rose. No one snuck in here wearing a mask and a hoodie. I don't blame you for imagining it, but no one was there."

Rose pursed her lips. "I know what I saw, Spence."

He kissed her the top of her head. "I think you need to get some rest today. Let's go home."

Later that day, Rose sat next to Spencer on the faded loveseat in her family room, holding his hand. As they sat there in silence, her anxiety built more and more. Her parents and Spencer's mom, Fiona, sat on the larger couch across from them. Rose didn't know why their parents wanted to talk to them together, but she suspected it couldn't be good.

Her dad spoke up first. "Rose, Spencer . . . I'm sure you're both wondering what we wanted to talk about. After all that's happened the past few weeks, we don't think it's safe for us to stay in town for the time being. The police are working diligently to find the culprit, but until they're caught, we don't feel safe here. We installed cameras at each entry point to the house, and we're having an alarm technician come out tomorrow to install a security alarm."

Spencer raised his eyebrows at Rose, then turned back to their parents. "What are we going to do, then? Where will we go?"

Rose's mom spoke up to answer them. "We think it's best if we leave town for a while. We're renting an Airbnb forty-five minutes away. It's not too far, but far enough that we should have the target off our backs. We'll stay there for the rest of the summer. Don't tell anyone where we're going. And there will be strict rules for you two going forwa—"

Rose cut her off. "An Airbnb?" She nervously squeezed Spencer's hand. "What rules?"

But Spencer interjected before Rose could get an answer. "What precautions are we taking, Mom? Shouldn't we get cameras and an alarm too?"

Rose's dad gestured to Fiona. "Spencer, I'm helping your mom install cameras too. You and Rose are always together, and with you two . . . ahem . . . dating now, you may be a target as well. They already went after Kasey, so they may be attacking anyone close to Rose."

Rose narrowed her eyes. "Why do you think they're going after people close to me? Is there something you aren't telling us? Were the police able to identify someone?"

Rose's dad ran a hand through his close-cropped, dark brown hair. "When your sister went missing . . ." He paused, blinking rapidly as if he was trying not to cry. "Your mom and I received a note signed by The Midnight Flower. We thought it was a joke or someone toying with us about your sister. We handed the note over to the police, but nothing ever came of it. I had almost forgotten about it until you thought you saw an intruder outside your bedroom back in June."

Rose swore her heart nearly stopped beating at her dad's admission. "Did the police ever give it back?"

Her mom shook her head, putting her hand on her dad's shoulder. "No, they kept it because the investigation is still ongoing, technically. Although there haven't been any new leads in months."

Rose let go of Spencer's hand, jumped up from the couch, and forced herself to ask the burning question pounding in her head. "So, you think The Midnight Flower is the one who took Lily?"

Her dad swallowed hard, his gaze unwavering, even after keeping this secret from his daughter for all this time. "Yes, Rose, we think The Midnight Flower is the one who took your sister."

"Mom, Dad . . . there's something else I have to tell you. I've been receiving notes all summer from The Midnight Flower," Rose said. "Do you know if Lily ever received notes signed with that name?"

Her dad grimaced. "As far as we know, she didn't, but clearly, neither of our daughters share important details of their lives with us."

Rose's face fell. "I'm sorry for not telling you sooner. It sounds stupid, but I—I didn't want you to worry about me more than you already were."

Rose's mom laughed, the sound manic and loud. "You're our daughter, Rose. We won't ever stop worrying about you! It's our job to keep you safe."

Rose and Spencer filled in their parents with as much information as they had about The Midnight Flower. Rose's dad called the police to see if any of it would help them identify a suspect. He insisted that they interrogate anyone Rose and Lily had close contact with. Someone who could have stalked both of them.

Rose and Spencer had already suspected that her anonymous stalker was the same person who took her sister, but to hear from her parents that they had known for a year the nickname of the person who supposedly took Lily . . . it was horrifying.

Had The Midnight Flower been stalking Lily too?

Chapter 44: Rose

Rose's parents told her to pack and be ready to leave in the morning after the security alarm was installed. They planned to set the alarm, test the new cameras, and leave for the Airbnb soon after. Rose pulled a suitcase out of her closet and stuffed it full of clothes, her swimsuit, a few books, and toiletries.

Hesitating, she unlocked her desk drawer and slid out the notes from The Midnight Flower, along with her notebook and list of suspects. If she was going to be gone for the rest of the summer, the evidence might come in handy.

Rose needed to read the first note from The Midnight Flower—the one they sent when Lily was taken. Rose suspected this was all part of a larger scheme. Had The Midnight Flower stalked Lily too? Was that the real reason Lily followed Rose and Spencer into the woods a year ago? If she was scared and didn't want to be alone, even in the safety of her own room, she might have followed them to tell them what was going on. Lily didn't have many friends, so she must have wanted Rose's help. After all, Rose was her big sister, so why wouldn't she trust her?

Rose fought the nearly overwhelming urge to cry yet again over the loss of her sister and how it truly was all her fault. For a year, the guilt had been eating her up inside. If she could find out who The Midnight Flower was and what they wanted from her and Lily, then she could get vengeance for her sister. It was too late to save Lily, but she would do her damn best to atone for her sins.

Sleep was impossible that night, so Rose sat at her desk searching the internet with any combination of words she could think of pertaining to The Midnight Flower. Nothing useful popped up, except a comic book character, but none of it was relevant to her or Lily. She stopped typing and pondered the keyword combination again. She searched Lily's name. Missing persons notices popped up, but there wasn't an obituary. Even after months had passed and everyone was certain Lily wasn't alive anymore, her parents hadn't wanted to have a funeral. That would mean giving up on their daughter, and they couldn't do that. They could barely acknowledge that she was gone.

Yawning, Rose shut her laptop and pushed it away from her. She dug underneath her desk for her laptop bag and slid the laptop inside. When it was closed, she set it next to her suitcase and stared at her pile of belongings.

When was the last time she had gone into Lily's room? Her mom went in there once a week to dust and vacuum, and sometimes Rose heard her in there crying. Lily's room was right next to hers. Other than that, she didn't think anyone went in there. It was too sad, too difficult to be reminded of the wonderful girl who had been stolen from them much too young.

Turning her bedroom doorknob as quietly as possible, Rose tiptoed to the next room and steeled herself. Going into her dead sister's bedroom would be difficult, but not impossible. She could do this. For Lily.

She opened the door, which squeaked slightly from lack of use. Rose darted a glance down the hall toward her parents' bedroom, but no one stirred. She snuck into Lily's room and shut the door, praying it didn't squeak again. When she was safely inside the room, she studied the space, picturing Lily sitting on the twin-sized bed with her wavy, red hair in her typical braid, her green eyes shining as she listened to one of Rose's stories.

Rose patted the bed gently, the flower-covered quilt perfectly straight, with three pillows propped against the headboard. A pile of stuffed animals sat on the bed like a small army. The walls were painted pink and covered in boy band posters. Against the wall, there was a small, white desk similar to the one in Rose's room. Over the desk, a corkboard had a few photos pinned to it. One of Lily and Rose on a family vacation visiting their grandparents in Minnesota. The last professional family photo they had taken, only months before Lily disappeared. Lily and Rose eating ice cream cones hilariously big for them when they were much smaller. Lily and Rose with their arms wrapped around each other, standing in front of their brand-new bikes. All the photos were of Rose and her sister. Lily didn't really have any friends.

Tears fell steadily as Rose gazed at the photos. Why hadn't she been nicer to her sister? Why had she treated Lily like she was a nuisance? If she had let her sister stay with her and Spencer in the woods that night... If she hadn't banished her and told her to go home... Leaving her to walk home by herself at night... Their lives would be so much different now. She wouldn't be consumed with guilt and sadness. Instead, she would be sitting in Lily's room, eating cookies they had snuck out of the kitchen and giggling while hoping their parents didn't wake up.

She placed a palm on the desk, averting her eyes from the photos. They were too painful to continue looking at, but maybe Lily had left behind something that could be helpful. Where would she hide a secret, something she didn't want anyone else to find?

Rose opened every drawer of the desk, unearthing old homework, report cards full of A's, and assorted pens and markers. Nothing juicy.

Leaning back against the desk, she pushed the desk chair away and ducked under the desk. There was a small fuzzy rug. With a blast of inspiration, she also moved that aside and gasped when an eight-by-eight photo box peeked out from underneath it. She didn't know what was inside the box, but she was certain it didn't contain photos.

Rose pushed the box out from under the desk, moved the fuzzy rug back to its original spot, and crawled out. But she stood up too soon and slammed her head against the desk.

"Fuck!" she yelled, holding her head and grimacing.

Of course, she had hit her head after her traumatic head injury only yesterday. It made the pain much worse than it normally would have been.

Panicking about her parents waking up, she picked up the photo box and snuck back into her own bedroom. She zipped the photo box into her suitcase. As the adrenaline wore off, she finally slipped into bed, too tired to worry about the box's contents until the next day.

Chapter 45: Rose

Pulling the lid off the photo box, a neat stack of letters was revealed. Spencer gasped as Rose picked up the letters and set them on the middle of the rug. She unfolded one and quickly scanned it to read the signature at the end, boldly proclaiming it was from The Midnight Flower.

"Spence, they're all from The Midnight Flower. Whoever he is, he was stalking Lily and sending notes to her too," Rose whispered, not wanting her parents or Fiona to hear them.

"What does it mean, though? Why would he go after Lily? We thought he was going after you because he knew our secret—that we were with Lily that night and told her to go home by herself—but if he was stalking Lily first . . . What did he want from her? She was only a kid." Spencer's hazel eyes were wide with horror.

"I don't know what it means, but it's not good."

"We need to figure out who this creep is," Spencer said, moving closer to her and peering over her shoulder to examine the letters.

Rose leaned back against Spencer so she was lying against his chest. "And why he went after my sister and now me. What does he want with us? Why did he pick us?"

Rose turned her head to face him and curled up against his chest, wanting comfort and safety, but she didn't know if she would feel safe ever again. Even if they could figure out who The Midnight Flower was, they would still have to stop him and make sure he was arrested. Would that be enough, though? Someone like that wouldn't atone for their crimes. She wanted more than jail for him. Rose wanted him dead, and she wanted to be the one to kill him.

Spencer held her arms gently and kissed her on the top of her head. He must have noticed she was trembling; although it wasn't from fear, it was from her thinly veiled rage.

"Hey, it will be okay. We left town for a reason. We're safe here. No one except our parents knows we're here. The Midnight Flower can't find us."

"I hope so." Rose hesitated, looking back up at Spencer at last. "Should we read the letters? It might help us find out more about The Midnight Flower. Maybe there's a clue that will point us in the right direction."

"Yeah, absolutely." Spencer reached for the first letter, unfolded it, and set it on the rug in front of them so they could both read it at the same time.

Lily,

Our love will stand the test of time. I knew you were the right choice as my partner, my perfect flower. Together, we can do anything—take down this town first, then the world. Love truly conquers all.

The Midnight Flower

Rose laid out the other notes, so they could easily flip through them and read the rest. Maybe they weren't in a particular order. They weren't dated, so she wasn't sure how to tell which one came first.

My perfect flower,

I promise you the world—everything you want is yours for the taking. I can give you anything. Can anyone else do that for you? Rose doesn't matter to me anymore. She meant nothing to me compared to you. What do I have to do to prove it to you? Do you want me to get rid of her? Just say the word and I'll do whatever you want.
The Midnight Flower

My perfect flower,
Run away with me. I promise I'll take you away from all this—the misery of this town and these small-minded people. They won't understand our love. I want to be with you and only you. Join me?
The Midnight Flower

Lily,
I'm watching you. I know every move you make, every person you talk to, every sin you commit. If you tell anyone about us, I promise you'll regret it.
The Midnight Flower

Lily,
This is your last warning. If you tell your parents or Rose, or if you go to the police, you'll never be seen or heard from again. Do you really think anyone will care? No one will miss you. I'm the only who understands you, the only one who truly cares. I'm all you need.
The Midnight Flower

"Whoa," Spencer said, setting the last letter aside.

Rose still felt like it was all sinking in. "Okay, let's take notes and piece together whatever we can from these letters." She rummaged around in her suitcase and pulled out her notebook and a pen.

"Right. So Lily was clearly dating someone who was manipulating her. Someone who had a vendetta against you? Someone you scorned?"

Spencer suggested.

"Hmm, maybe an ex? But why would they want to date Lily? And why would they kill her if they loved her?"

"From the letters, it sounds like Lily was thinking about turning him in. She might have told him she would go to the police or tell someone what was going on. Then he panicked and made it look like she disappeared and destroyed all the evidence," Spencer said.

"The Midnight Flower could be someone in a position of power, an adult she trusted. Someone whose reputation would be ruined if people found out they were together," Rose said, tapping her pen against the notebook, her stomach turning queasy. "This letter says, 'I promise I'll take you away from all this—the misery of this town and these small-minded people. They won't understand our love.' If Lily was being manipulated by an adult, then they were at best taking advantage of an underage girl, and at worst . . ." Rose couldn't finish the thought, but she assumed Spencer knew what she was hinting.

"Yeah, either way, I think that clears up that it couldn't be one of your exes. You never dated anyone older. Plus, did you ever break up with someone and piss them off so much that they would turn around and date your sister, stalk both of you, kidnap Lily, and kill Kasey?" Spencer asked incredulously, throwing his arms up in the air.

Rose bit her lip. "No. I'm still stuck on who they could be. I can't think of anyone that fits the criteria." Rose scribbled in the notebook, adding in what they had found out so far. "Well, we know more than we did earlier, but it's not enough to nail someone down. Have you heard any details about Kasey's funeral?"

"Her mom posted on her social media earlier. The funeral will be held this weekend. They're encouraging her classmates and friends to go. I know we would have to go back to Spartanburg, but I think—"

Rose cut him off, already anticipating the next words out of his mouth. "We should go. Don't criminals sometimes return to the scene of the crime, or show up at funerals for the people they kill to see if they can get away with it? It's like a pride thing, showing they're so much smarter than the police. They like being crafty and seen as intelligent."

"I think you're right. We need to go to Kasey's funeral and watch out for The Midnight Flower."

"The only question is, will our parents let us leave?" Rose asked.

Chapter 46: Rose

Rose should have known their parents would be hesitant about them attending Kasey's funeral. Their parents didn't want Rose and Spencer to have another run-in with The Midnight Flower, but that was exactly why they wanted to go. They couldn't explain that to their parents, though. They would sound crazy, admitting they were going after someone dangerous, a murderer who was killing young girls in their small town. Who knew if he had killed others?

When Rose explained the police would be at the funeral keeping an eye out for the killer, her parents finally caved.

"What do we do now?" Spencer asked, turning to her for answers, as always.

"Prepare our plan of attack," Rose said, as if it was obvious.

Spencer groaned and put his face in his hands for a few seconds before he made eye contact with her again. "Seriously? Do we have to?"

Rose glared at him. "Do you really need to ask that? This might be our only chance. We're being forced to hide away in this Airbnb, where no one knows our location. We need to go to the funeral and hope we can confront them. If The Midnight Flower sees us, they might give us another note, or they might be surprised to see us and slip up and make a mistake. Maybe we'll get lucky. If we can get close enough, we can take off their mask and find out their identity."

"Oh my God, Rose! That's so dangerous! Are you sure you want to do this?" Spencer asked, sounding timid, his voice wavering uncertainly.

"Yup."

Why did she always have to be the one to talk him into dangerous situations?

"Fine, but I'm not going unless we have a solid plan," Spencer said, caving as she had known he would. He always gave in to her, even before they were dating.

"I've already thought about it. At the funeral, we'll stand near the back during the service so we can check out everyone coming into the church. We'll also be able to see if anyone leaves during the service or comes in late. Plus, we can sneak out if we need to. After the funeral, Kasey's parents are having a wake at their house, so we'll go to that too. We can chat with people we know and try to get information out of them," Rose explained.

"Shouldn't we bring a weapon?" Spencer asked.

"Spencer Fitzgerald, are you suggesting we bring weapons into a church?" Rose asked with a small smile. The first authentic smile she had worn in days.

"Uh, I guess so?"

"I'll bring my pepper spray. I usually carry it in my purse. Do you still have that pocketknife?"

"Yeah, but—"

"Then bring it with you. If you wear a blazer or a suit jacket, you can keep it in your pocket, and no one will ever know. It's not like they have metal detectors or security guards in churches," Rose said with a laugh.

"True. I guess it's a plan, then. But what do we do after we unmask The Midnight Flower? We can't take down someone that powerful without restraining them. And if all we have is pepper spray and a pocketknife, I don't think we stand much of a chance. Too bad there isn't someone else we can team up with," Spencer mused.

"Well, actually—" Rose said before Spencer interrupted.

"Uh oh, what now?"

"I was thinking about asking Mason to help us."

Spencer's face turned bright red, almost the same vibrant shade as her hair. "What!" he exploded. "I'm not letting that asshole get anywhere near you. Why would you want to involve him? We can't trust him."

"Trust me, I wouldn't ask him for help if I didn't think it was necessary. But you're right about us needing backup, and he's perfect."

"Why does it have to be him? Isn't there someone else we can ask?" Spencer groaned.

"Our friends are in short supply, and we're already down one person," she said as a quiet reminder. "Besides, he's strong and muscular. If anyone can take down The Midnight Flower, it's him."

"Great, so now I need to work out more so I look like Mason?" Spencer complained, narrowing his hazel eyes at her.

He sounded upset, and she knew he was feeling insecure. Mason was hot, so she didn't blame him. Even if he was a jerk.

"I don't have feelings for him anymore, not after how he disrespected me and acted weird about Lily."

Spencer pulled her onto his lap, cradling his face in her hands with such softness and genuine caring. "Then why do you want to be around him again? We never really talked about what happened between you and Mason, but I pieced some details together."

Rose shook her head. "I don't want to talk about that right now. Who else could we ask?"

"I don't know. What about Reggie or Kylar?" Spencer suggested.

"Oh, great, let's invite Holly too and make sure all my exes are there," Rose replied sarcastically.

"Not a bad idea. She's probably the scariest out of all of them,"

Spencer joked.

Rose leaned forward until her forehead touched Spencer's lightly. She put her hands on his shoulders and met his eyes with a gaze full of warmth. "I don't know about that. To me, being vulnerable like this is scarier than facing The Midnight Flower."

Spencer ran his hand down her neck and pulled her head closer to his, his lips brushing softly against hers. He pulled away just enough to ask, "Is this scary?"

Rose trembled as she wrapped her arms around his neck. "Yes."

"What about this?" he asked, pressing his lips to hers with a bit more force this time.

"I'm not sure. I need another kiss to decide," Rose teased him.

"That can be arranged," Spencer promised.

***

On Saturday morning, Rose and Spencer drove to Spartanburg for Kasey's funeral. The funeral didn't start until 1:00 p.m., so they had some time to kill. They wandered around the cemetery behind the church, holding hands and enjoying the beautiful summer day, instead of concentrating on the reason they were there. Flowers were in full bloom in South Carolina, and many of the tombstones had bouquets of fresh flowers in front of them.

"I wonder how many people will show up," Rose said.

"Hopefully not too many, so we can spot The Midnight Flower," Spencer replied.

Fifteen minutes remained until the service started, and people had started arriving.

Rose and Spencer went to Kasey's parents to give their condolences. They exchanged tearful hugs with Kasey's mom, who was crying uncontrollably. She seemed so thankful that two of Kasey's friends were there;

she had worried no one would show up.

But people did show up. At first, they slowly trickled in, but soon enough, there was barely room for the gathering crowd. Rose worried that they wouldn't be able to see The Midnight Flower if he came.

Spencer leaned in close to her and whispered, "Don't worry. If he doesn't show up, we'll come up with a new plan. It will be okay."

Rose didn't feel reassured. Instead, she was full of grief and anger for what The Midnight Flower had taken from her. He had robbed her of the innocence of childhood, and he might have done the same to Lily. Instilling fear, terror, and paranoia in someone was enough to make them age faster than they should. The more she thought about her younger sister being stalked, threatened, and kidnapped, the more her anger grew.

As the funeral service started, Rose clung to Spencer's arms, unable to hold herself together. Her gentle sobs were muffled in his chest. When the pastor mentioned Kasey's "premature death" and "a life well-lived," Rose broke down into full-blown crying. Thoughts of Lily's fate bombarded her. It was all too much.

After what felt like forever, the service ended. Kasey's mom had invited them to the wake at their house, so they planned on attending it. Although Rose didn't think The Midnight Flower would attend the wake—he would stick out too much. It would be easier for him to blend in here, with a crowd of people packed together.

People headed toward their cars, either going home or to Kasey's house for the wake. Rose and Spencer took their time leaving, not in a rush and still hoping to run in to The Midnight Flower.

Outside the church, the wind swirled around Rose and Spencer, stirring up stray leaves from the sidewalk and lifting them into the air. When the wind died down, a figure emerged—a mysterious person wearing a black hood and a mask covering their face. Their guess had been right. The Midnight Flower was there.

Chapter 47: Rose

The remaining people at the church fled to their cars, running away from the hooded figure. The two police officers stationed outside the church fought their way through the panicking crowd.

Tugging on Spencer's suit jacket, Rose desperately wanted his attention on The Midnight Flower. When she faced Spencer, she could tell he had seen the stalker too. His hand went to his pocket. She assumed he was making sure his pocketknife was still there. Without checking, Rose knew her pepper spray was in her purse. She always kept it there.

She pulled Spencer through the crowd. It only took seconds for Rose to lose track of The Midnight Flower. Spencer's fingers laced through hers. He shoved his way through the crowd forcefully. A black-hooded figure sped toward the parking lot. Letting go of Spencer's hand, she chased the stranger. All she cared about was catching up with him.

Spencer called out, "Rose, wait! Wait for me!"

Spencer wasn't an athlete; he was a stereotypical gamer. Rose could easily outrun him. She didn't want to put him in more danger than she already had. This didn't involve him. The Midnight Flower had taken her sister, so it was Rose's problem to deal with, not Spencer's. She couldn't bear her best friend being injured because of her carelessness.

She had lost enough people already. So she kept running, chasing The Midnight Flower, right on his heels.

Is this it? Is this the moment we've been waiting for?

The Midnight Flower turned around and faced her. Rose was barely a foot away from him. She studied the intricate details of the mask covering their face. This close to the stalker, something seemed off about them. Before, when she encountered The Midnight Flower, they were shorter than both her and Spencer. But now, they were much taller than her. How was that possible? The only plausible explanation Rose had come up with was that The Midnight Flower was more than one person.

"Rose, I assumed you would find me here," The Midnight Flower said in the familiar deep, husky voice.

"Who are you?" Rose asked, her hands balling into fists.

The Midnight Flower laughed, a harsh, grating sound. "All in due time, Rose. You haven't reached the last level of my little game yet. You're taking longer than I thought you would to solve this. A year has passed since your sister went missing. What have you been doing all this time? Sipping cheap wine coolers and breaking people's hearts?"

Spencer caught up to them and stood in front of Rose. "Stay away from us. I'm not afraid to hurt you," he warned.

"Oh, Spencer. What made you think threatening me was a good idea? You clearly don't know what I'm capable of. I suppose that means I need to make another show of power. Hmm . . ." The Midnight Flower paused, their head shifting from side to side as they scanned the area. "Ah, I spy a target."

Rose blinked, uncomprehending. Spencer grabbed her around the waist and held her back. The Midnight Flower darted over to where Mason was standing. Leaning against a massive oak tree by himself, his phone occupied his attention. Sneaking behind the tree, The Midnight Flower whipped out a knife. After several flashes of silver and garbled screams from Mason, Mason crumpled to the ground, his back pressed against the tree.

At the sound of the screams, the police came running toward them.

Rose fought Spencer and broke free from his grip. Meanwhile, The Midnight Flower ran off. Spencer went after him, while Rose went to Mason.

"Someone, help!" she yelled. "We need an ambulance!"

Pressing her hands to Mason's bloodied chest, she applied pressure to the wound, scanning her memories for anything remotely helpful in the situation.

"Rose . . . I—I thought I was safe," Mason choked out, struggling to breathe already.

"What do you mean?" Rose questioned, not caring that blood covered her hands.

"The Midnight . . . Flower. They tried to . . . to make me j-join."

"What?" Rose stared down at Mason. She fiercely tried to staunch the bleeding, but it was no use. She wasn't sure the ambulance would arrive in time. His face was becoming paler, almost a sickly gray.

"I s-said no. I c-couldn't hurt you . . . but they want . . . their r-revenge a-and . . ." Mason's eyes fluttered shut.

"Mason, no! What else did they tell you? Do you know who The Midnight Flower is? Why are they doing this?" Rose cried out.

Tears fell freely down her cheeks. Streaks of mascara and eyeliner mixed with her tears. She didn't care about her appearance anymore. She only cared about learning the truth. Why did The Midnight Flower kill Mason?

Mason took a shuddering breath, but his eyes remained closed. "Take m-my ph-phone," he whispered in a strained voice.

Rose dug around in both of his suit coat pockets before she found it. She snatched the phone and slid it into her purse before anyone noticed. She didn't want the police to find out and take the phone. Several people were milling around nearby. One of them had called 911 when Rose yelled for help, but the ambulance still wasn't there. Rose remained kneeling next to her ex-crush's body, wondering if he was dead but too terrified to check for a pulse and find out.

A police officer knelt beside her, telling her he would take it from there. Relief flickered through her. Mason was dead, but at least the cops could handle the situation.

With a sudden crack of fear, she whipped her head around, searching for Spencer. She hadn't seen him in at least ten minutes, since—

Since he went after The Midnight Flower by himself.

And now, he was nowhere to be found.

Chapter 48: Rose

The police insisted on questioning Rose. She had stayed by Mason's side the entire time, so the police wanted to know what she saw and if she knew who the mysterious killer was. Rose wished she had more answers, but she relayed as much as she could to the police, hoping it would be enough for them to solve the case. When Rose brought up Kasey's murder and Lily's disappearance, the police officer interviewing her became uninterested. In other words, they didn't believe her that the cases were connected.

In a town this small, it was ridiculous to think that there were multiple murderers running rampant. Wasn't that much more terrifying than one person murdering several people? Or was it less terrifying? Rose didn't have a good gauge for that sort of thing anymore after losing her sister, her friend, and her former crush. She wasn't sure how much more she could handle.

When the questioning ended, Rose asked the police officers if they had seen Spencer. None of the funeral-goers remained. The police had sent everyone home and cordoned off the cemetery since it was now a crime scene. Panicking, she pulled out her cell phone from her purse and dialed his number. It rang for a few seconds before Spencer answered.

"Spence! Thank God you're okay. I was so worried," Rose said, the words coming out all in one breath because she was so relieved. She held her hand to her chest, praying her heart rate would return to normal now that she knew Spencer was okay.

"Hello, Rose. This isn't Spencer. Guess again," a deep, husky voice said.

Rose's heart plummeted into her stomach. "How did you get his phone? Where is he?"

Her eyes darted to the police officer climbing into his police car. Should she stop him from leaving and tell him that she couldn't find Spencer? Or would the officer think she was paranoid and tell her to go home?

"Don't go getting any wild ideas. If you tell the police, you'll regret it. I know all your secrets, Rose, enough to ruin your life. In fact, I may be the only other person who knows the truth about the night Lily disappeared and why it's all your fault . . ." The Midnight Flower said.

Rose froze. She had already talked to the police and told them—well, not *everything*, but enough that The Midnight Flower would be angry if they knew. Had she screwed up any chance of finding out her sister's fate? And saving her best friend?

"Hello? Rose, are you still there?" The Midnight Flower asked in a tone laced with irritation.

Rose gripped her cell phone tightly against her ear, straining not to lose it. It was obvious in her shaky voice as she replied, but she didn't care. She needed Spencer to be all right. This was what she had wanted to avoid. If Spencer died, it would be her fault.

"Yes, I'm still here. What do you want from me?" she asked in a breathless voice, unable to breathe deeply enough.

Her legs trembled while she stood backed against a tree, waiting for their answer.

"I want what I've always wanted. I want you to apologize for what you did to me. You at least owe me that much. After everything you did, the way you destroyed my life... It's the bare minimum for human decency."

But Rose didn't know what they meant and couldn't apologize if she didn't know who they were.

"Who are you?" she asked. Rose wrinkled her brow as she pondered their identity.

"I'm hurt, Rose. After everything I've revealed, all my letters and clues, you still don't remember what you did to me? How could you forget something so awful? You have until Sunday at midnight to find Spencer. Otherwise, he'll be the next death you're responsible for."

"Wait! How do I know where to find him? You haven't told me anything!" Rose screeched.

The line beeped. Rose pulled her phone away from her face and was disheartened to see the call had ended. Trembling, she debated calling her parents. She noticed the police officer she talked to had left the cemetery, although detectives and crime scene investigators had cordoned off the area where Mason was killed. It was an active crime scene, so she should leave. The only problem was that she couldn't go home, and she couldn't return to the Airbnb without Spencer. To say their parents would be livid was an understatement.

Rose powered down her cell phone, realizing her best option was to cut off all communication, so her parents couldn't ask where she was when they noticed she was gone too long. They wouldn't be able to track her, either.

She needed to find Spencer, and this time, she knew exactly whom to turn to.

Chapter 49: Rose

It was official: Rose was on her own. With Spencer gone, she didn't have many options. She had driven aimlessly around town, guessing about the location The Midnight Flower could have taken Spencer. She still didn't know who they were, so how was she supposed to find him?

Her next move had come down to one fact—she needed back-up. She couldn't do this on her own. The only other people who could help weren't exactly her favorite people on the planet, but they might help her if they knew she was desperate. She didn't relish the idea of asking for help, but she was smart enough to know that going after the mysterious, masked stranger by herself wouldn't end well. That was horror movie survival 101: never go into battle alone, especially without telling someone where you're going.

But first, Rose needed to go through Mason's phone. With his dying breath, he had told her to take it, so there must be important information on it. Something that could help her find out who The Midnight Flower was. Mason told her The Midnight Flower tried to enlist him, so this solidified her theory that they were more than one person. They were recruiting others. Why had they wanted Mason to join their team? What did they want from Rose? She was still unsure what their goal was and how it related to her sister. If they were intent on getting revenge on Rose, then it must be because they had dated.

Had they tried to recruit Spencer too, then?

No, that's silly. He would have told me.

But would he? If Spencer was trying to protect Rose, he might have hidden it from her. After all, she had a few secrets of her own Spencer didn't know about. Regardless, she needed to get ready, so she didn't go into a dangerous situation unprepared.

Swiping up on Mason's phone, Rose was surprised to find that it wasn't password protected. He might have foreseen his fate and known he would need to give his phone to Rose. Otherwise, why wouldn't he keep his phone secure, especially if there was information related to The Midnight Flower on it?

Not knowing what she was searching for, Rose went to Mason's texts. She didn't think he was dumb enough to name a contact "The Midnight Flower," so she searched for any names that seemed fake or out of place. He only had a handful of text chains saved, so that helped. With a pang, she saw the texts she had sent him were still saved on his phone. Besides that, he had texts from his mom and younger brother, some guys on the football team, a girl who was probably his new fling, and—

Rose's heart nearly stopped at the last name in his recent text messages. A name that shot tendrils of uncertainty and anxiety through her chest.

Kylar.

***

Fuming, Rose drove straight to Kylar's house, which was in the neighborhood next to hers. She parked her car in the street and banged on his front door until the door opened a minute later.

Kylar stood in the doorway, glowering at her, his dark brown hair wet like he had just taken a shower. Was it her imagination, or did his face look pale? Was his anger all an act? Why would he be so mad at her? They had broken up ages ago, after all. There was no way he cared about that anymore. They had only dated for a few months during their freshman year of high school.

"Why are you here?" Kylar asked in a deep, husky voice that was all too familiar.

Rose stared at him, barely breathing. During their brief run-in at the coffee shop weeks ago, they hadn't said more than five words to each other. Kylar had told her he was getting over a cold, but maybe he had pretended so she didn't recognize his voice. Now it was all too obvious.

"We need to talk, Kylar."

She had screwed up by coming to his house without thinking it through, but it was too late. She didn't believe Kylar would do this to her. Denial sprinkled over her like a light rainfall. Kylar couldn't be The Midnight Flower. He just couldn't. When they dated, he had always been so sweet to her. He couldn't be the same person stalking her and harassing her. He couldn't have taken Lily . . .

Kylar remained in the doorway, unmoving, but she thought he wouldn't hurt her, so she shoved past him into his house.

"Is anyone home? Your sister or your parents?"

"No. My sister is a camp counselor at a theater camp for the summer. My parents are both at work," he murmured, thinking through each word.

He had always been like that. He was the opposite of her in so many ways, which was why she had broken up with him. Their personalities didn't mesh well, but that didn't mean she had wanted to hurt him.

Rose stormed into the kitchen, pulling out a chair and gesturing for Kylar to sit down. She sat in the chair across from him. "Do you know why I'm here?"

She saw him visibly swallow and nod.

"I came here from Kasey's funeral." She narrowed her eyes at him.

"Were you there?"

"No, I went for a run to decompress. I just got out of the shower. Sorry about Kasey. I—"

"You're sorry that you killed my friend?" Rose snorted derisively. "I don't have time for your games or your fake apologies. Where's Spencer?"

Kylar squinted at her as if he was confused. "Why would I know where Spencer is? Isn't he your best friend?"

"What do you mean? Are you messing with me, Kylar?"

Kylar shook his head, his wet hair sending tiny droplets of water across the kitchen table. "I don't know what you're talking about."

"But aren't you... You're working with The Midnight Flower, right?" Rose asked, suddenly unsure of her assumptions.

Kylar's face paled even more. He shrank down in his chair for a few seconds before he sprang up, his green eyes searching around the kitchen nervously. "All I did was make the phone calls and show up when he wanted me to give you a note. I didn't hurt anyone, I swear." Then he added in a mumble, "And I made the smoke bombs."

"Well, I guess chemistry was always your strong suit," Rose replied with a snort.

"Rose, you need to leave. I'm not messing around. It isn't safe for you to be here. If they find out we're talking—"

"Then what? They'll kill us? I think they're already planning to kill me. They have Spencer. I need to find him before it's too late." Tears fell from her eyes, dripping down her cheeks and splashing onto the table. "I can't lose him, Kylar. He's all I have left."

Kylar's face fell. "Okay. I get why you chose him."

Rose sniffled, attempting to rein in her emotions. "What do you mean?"

"You never really loved me. You always loved him," Kylar said simply.

Rose dug her nails into her palms, reflecting on her past relationships.

Maybe that was why all her other relationships had failed. She wouldn't admit it out loud—that would be cruel to her ex—but Kylar was right. It had been Spencer all along.

Instead, she replied in as kind of a tone as possible, "I cared about you, Kylar. I still do. I don't understand why you're doing this. Before Mason died, he gave me his phone. I found texts you sent him."

This time, Kylar's face reddened, and his hands balled into fists by his sides. "Mason is dead because he wouldn't listen! He was an idiot. All he had to do was obey The Midnight Flower, and they would have let him go eventually. He screwed up by dating you and getting too close to you. It may not have seemed like it, but he cared about you in his own twisted way."

Rose pursed her lips. "Mason kept bringing up Lily. It was like he was obsessed with her, with finding out more about what happened. I don't think he ever cared about me. If he was working for The Midnight Flower this whole time, then it all makes sense."

"You don't understand their motivation. You—"

"I don't understand any of this!" Rose exploded, throwing her arms up in the air and standing from her chair. "Explain it to me, so I understand. Please," she said in a softer tone, hoping she could appeal to the part of Kylar who had once loved her.

Kylar shook his head, turning away from her. "I wish I could, but I can't. It goes against the rules. You need to go before they find out you were here." He scanned the room again. "If they haven't already."

"What will happen if they find out? Who are they, Kylar? Please help me find Spencer. I promise I'll help you get out of this mess too. It isn't too late for you to turn your life around."

"Really? You would help me, even after knowing I've been involved?" Kylar's green eyes appeared hopeful as he took a step closer to her.

"Of course. I want all of us to escape and stop being terrorized by The Midnight Flower. They need to be stopped. Don't you see that? You aren't unreasonable. You must know how this has affected me," Rose pleaded.

The sound of glass shattering interrupted their conversation. Rose turned around. Shards of glass scattered across the ceramic tiles. A gaping hole in the sliding door led out to the patio, and a smoke bomb appeared. Plumes of grayish-black smoke erupted. Rose screamed, diving away from the door. Glass crunched under the soles of her shoes.

"Rose, get out of here!" Kylar yelled.

Rose couldn't see him through the smoke. The smoke thickened in the small space. It spread throughout the lower level of the house. Rose coughed. Covering her mouth and nose with her sleeve, she headed for the front door.

"Kylar, where are you?"

"It's not safe. Rose, please leave. Get out of here! The Midnight Flower is here!" Kylar yelled again.

Rose stumbled through the fog with one arm covering her mouth and the other braced in front of her to feel for any obstacles. The fog was thick and made it difficult to breathe normally. She wasn't sure how long she could continue before her oxygen ran out. Blindly, she kept moving until she reached the front door after what felt like hours, but it couldn't have been more than a few minutes.

She turned the doorknob and escaped the smoke, breathing in deep gulps of fresh air as she stepped outside. Rose sprinted to her car, not looking back as she jumped into the driver's seat and drove away. She didn't want to think about whether Kylar was okay or if The Midnight Flower was after her; she just knew she needed to get somewhere safe.

Chapter 50: Rose

One year ago

Breathing hard, Rose stood with her back pressed against her bedroom door. She had just finished talking to the police. Two days had crept by since Lily went missing. Rose and Spencer had agreed not to tell anyone that they saw Lily that night—it was for the best if no one knew Rose had yelled at her and told her to go home alone so late.

Rose had assumed—stupidly, maybe—that Lily would have shown up by now and that she would return home safely. But she was still missing. Her parents were both a wreck. She didn't know how her family would get through this if they didn't find Lily. But what was the alternative? Rose couldn't comprehend the possibility of her sister not being found alive and well. This wasn't a normal worry for an almost fifteen-year-old, but it was her own fault, she reminded herself.

If only she had let Lily hang out with her and Spencer that night.

Or offered to walk her home.

Or literally done anything else besides scream at her to leave and send her off into the dangerous darkness by herself.

That night would haunt her forever.

Rose didn't know where Lily was, but the police assumed she had been kidnapped. They lived in a relatively small, safe town, but their town wasn't immune to horrible acts. A child could be kidnapped anywhere, even from the yard of a friend's house like Kara Robinson, or from their own front yard like Sofia Silva. It wasn't unheard of. What Rose, her parents, and the police were stuck on, though, was who would take Lily.

As far as everyone knew, she had never dated or shown any strange interests in someone older or in a position of authority. They all assumed it must have been a stranger, someone who went after young girls and targeted Lily.

Rose pondered two questions over and over as time passed. Who took her sister? And what did they want?

***

Present day

Over the past year, Rose had debated often whether her sister was still alive. As she came closer to uncovering the sordid truth, she wasn't sure she wanted to know anymore. What if Lily was dead? Finding that out would only hurt her and her parents even more. She didn't know if she could do that to them. Was it better if Lily was gone forever? Or to hold on to false hope and never know for sure?

Pulling into the parking lot of a clothing store downtown, she parked her car, then inspected the parking lot. She didn't think anyone had followed her, but The Midnight Flower had been watching her all summer. Just because Rose hadn't seen them didn't mean they weren't lurking nearby. They had to be adept at remaining invisible, otherwise how had they gone undetected for so long?

Rose pulled out her cell phone, pausing as she debated whom to turn to next. Kylar was involved with The Midnight Flower, either working for him willingly or being blackmailed into acting as his lackey. She could call Reggie or Holly. She wasn't a fan of either of those options, but they might help. Kylar and Reggie had been friends at one point—well, before she dumped Kylar for Reggie. It wasn't her finest moment.

***

Freshman year – November

Kylar stared at her, uncomprehending. His green eyes became wide and glassy as the reality of Rose's words hit him.

"I'm really sorry, Kylar. I never wanted to hurt you. I still care about—"

Kylar laughed and brushed a hand through his dark brown hair that stopped above his shoulders. "Too late, Rose. I don't think you ever cared about me. It's because of Reggie, isn't it?"

Rose's gaze dropped to the textbook on the desk in front of her. They were in the Chemistry classroom because it was empty during their lunch.

Kylar snorted. "Fine, you don't have to confirm it. Maybe I should warn him that you'll leave him in three months for someone else."

The words stung, but Rose deserved it. Kylar was so nice. He had always treated her well. But Kylar was on the debate team, and he was too quiet. Reggie was an athlete. He was tall and muscular, with slicked-back, dark brown hair and brown eyes that were always full of mischief and danger. From the second his eyes met hers, she couldn't resist.

He stood from the desk next to her and narrowed his eyes. "And in case it wasn't obvious, I'm not helping you with your chemistry homework anymore."

Present day

Rose turned her phone back on and sent a quick text to Holly, deciding that contacting her was marginally better than Reggie. After all, Holly had been creeping on her Instagram and liked one of her old photos a week and a half ago. That had to mean something. Reggie would lord it over her forever if she asked for help.

> **Rose:** Hi, Holly. I'm in a dangerous situation and I need your help. Can you meet me downtown?

> **Holly:** Sure. Be there in 10 minutes.

It surprised her that Holly had responded so quickly, but it was summer, after all. She must not have much going on. Rose sat in her car, struggling to figure out how to summarize what had happened. What could she tell her, and what was better left unsaid?

Ten minutes later, Holly texted her again.

> **Holly:** I'm by the ice cream place we used to go to. Meet me out front.

> **Rose:** K, on my way.

Rose turned off her cell phone again, locked her car, and headed for the ice cream shop. She didn't want her parents to track her. As her cell phone powered down, she realized with a shock that she rarely, if ever, turned her phone off. Not only that, but she frequently posted photos on social media and checked into locations online. She had made it all too easy for The Midnight Flower to track her movements.

When she reached her destination, she found Reggie standing outside waiting for her with his arm wrapped around the waist of the gorgeous blonde she had asked for help. *Holly.*

Gritting her teeth, she approached them both, eyeing Reggie the entire way. "I wasn't expecting to see you here." She turned to Holly. "I thought we were meeting alone."

Holly fake pouted, pushing out her red lips. "I was with Reggie when you texted me. I couldn't leave him in bed alone." She batted her eyelashes at Rose.

"Hi, Rose. I thought you wouldn't mind if I was here too. It sounded like an emergency," Reggie said in his gruff voice.

Rose rolled her eyes, knowing Holly was trying to bait her. Her two exes dating was fantastic, and the fact that she needed their help to save her new boyfriend was *even more* fantastic.

Chapter 51: Rose

"We need to talk somewhere private." Rose's gaze drifted across the outside of the ice cream shop, the coffee shop down the road, and the boutique clothing stores. "There are too many witnesses here."

Reggie's dark brown eyes darkened until they were nearly black. "Why? What's going on?"

Holly glared at Reggie and beckoned for Rose to follow her. "Come on, I know a place."

Hesitantly, Rose and Reggie followed Holly past the crowds and the hustle and bustle of downtown, toward a wooded area. They stopped near an abandoned park that Rose hadn't known existed. The swings creaked eerily in the summer breeze, the hinges rusty and unoiled. The slide appeared decrepit, with a crack down the center, as if it could split in two at any moment. There wasn't much else besides monkey bars and two wooden picnic tables.

Holly led them to a picnic table and sat down. "No one ever comes here. It's an old park from the early 2000s. The mayor keeps claiming he'll fix it up, but he never does, so no one brings their kids here. It's not exactly safe," Holly explained.

Rose and Reggie stared at Holly. Rose wondered how Holly knew about this place. She assumed Reggie was wondering the same thing.

Holly put her hands on her tiny hips. "I like to come here by myself and think, okay?"

Rose couldn't picture her evil ex thinking about anything besides drama and secrets, so she couldn't help the snort that came out.

"Why did you text me? We aren't friends anymore. Don't you have someone else to turn to?" Holly asked.

"I wish I did, but considering my sister is missing, Kasey and Mason were murdered, and Spencer was kidnapped . . . No, I don't think there is anyone left I can ask. I can't tell my parents what's going on. You cared about me at one point, so I thought maybe you still do. I guess I was wrong," Rose said sarcastically, doing her best to not let repeating the traumatic events get to her. This was hard enough to go through without being constantly reminded of what she had been through.

"Oh my God," Holly said, her mouth dropping open. "Mason and Spencer too?" she asked in disbelief.

Numbly, Rose nodded, confirming Holly's question. "Spencer and I went to Kasey's funeral. We saw The Midnight Flower. He stabbed Mason and killed him." A sob escaped from her throat, unbidden. "By the time I finished talking to the police about what happened, Spencer had disappeared. I couldn't find him. Then I received a phone call from his phone, but it wasn't him. It was The Midnight Flower. He told me he took Spencer and that I have until midnight on Sunday to find him. I know it's not much to go off of, but—"

Rose had planned to pull out her bag to show them Mason's phone, the texts from Kylar proving he was working with The Midnight Flower, and the letters Lily had received from The Midnight Flower, but her bag was gone. She must have left it in Kylar's house in her haste to escape the smoke bomb and potential death.

That could only mean one thing—The Midnight Flower had all her evidence.

Rose witnessed Holly and Reggie exchanging a concerned glance.

"Fuck," she muttered to herself.

"What's wrong?" Holly asked, batting her enticing blue eyes at her.

Rose scuffed her boot in the dirt. "I must have left my stuff in Kylar's house."

"Are you sure? We could go over there and get it back," Holly offered. "We'll go with you."

"Um, I don't know about that. The Midnight Flower threw a rock or something through the sliding glass door with a smoke bomb. I think he was trying to hurt us or warn us not to team up against him," Rose said. "It's probably not smart to go back there. Kylar basically admitted to working with him."

"You're right about part of that," Reggie said with a sigh, running his hand through his artfully slicked-back, slightly tousled hair.

"What do you mean?" Rose scrunched up her nose in confusion.

"The Midnight Flower doesn't want you talking to Kylar, but he doesn't want you talking to us, either. He'll be here any minute," Reggie said, shoving his phone back into his jeans pocket.

Rose's heart nearly stilled. "Wh-what? Are you working for him too?" She whipped her head to the side to face Holly. "And you too, Holly?" Her voice cracked as she asked the second question.

Rose hadn't explained to them who The Midnight Flower was, or told them about the threatening, anonymous letters. They had already known because they must be working with him. Had everyone she ever loved betrayed her? Was this all some kind of sick joke? She didn't think she could handle any more heartbreak or bad news.

"Yes," Holly said in a tone that sounded almost sorrowful. She shrugged her shoulders. "When The Midnight Flower approached me and asked me to join, he made a very compelling offer. It would have been stupid to refuse." A Cheshire-like grin spread across her angelic face.

"But . . . why?" Rose asked, unable to comprehend what was happening.

Reggie and Holly were both sitting across from her at the picnic table. They were in a wooded area at an abandoned park, with no one else around. She couldn't hear the sounds of downtown anymore—cars driving by, children squealing for ice cream, dogs barking. It was almost completely silent. And that unnerved her more than anything when it finally hit her how stupid this decision had been to come here with them alone.

Without her bag, she didn't have her pepper spray. She wouldn't be able to fight them off—Holly, maybe, but Reggie was muscular and a star athlete, so he was in shape.

"You didn't think you would get away with dumping so many people without any consequences, did you? If I couldn't have you, then I didn't want anyone to. You had the best, and you settled for trash." Reggie's dark eyes glimmered threateningly.

Rose gripped the edges of the picnic table, fighting off the waves of nausea pulsing through her body. This couldn't be happening. She had known they might be against helping her, but this—this was not at all like what she had expected. For two people she had once cared for so deeply to completely and utterly betray her . . .

Even more than she wanted to understand why they had committed these horrific acts against her and decided to serve The Midnight Flower in the name of revenge, she had another question that was more pressing. If she wanted to save Spencer and find out her sister's fate, she needed to know the truth once and for all.

"Do you know who The Midnight Flower is?"

Chapter 52: Rose

Holly blinked at her, her mascaraed eyelashes long and dark. Rose tried not to gawk, but it was impossible not to get lost in those blue eyes. Even if Holly was a royal bitch who had betrayed her, she was still beautiful.

Holly glanced sideways at Reggie before answering. Reggie simply shrugged his massive shoulders.

"Yes, we know who he is," Holly said at last.

Rose gasped, unable to contain her shock. She was so close to getting some answers. "Can you take me to him?" she pleaded, leaning over the picnic table closer to Holly and Reggie.

This time, Reggie was the one who spoke. "Yeah." He pulled out his phone, and his fingers flew across the screen while he typed.

Rose assumed he was texting The Midnight Flower and waited patiently for him to speak again.

Reggie glanced up from his phone. "He says it's time for you to meet him. Let's go."

Holly stood and practically bounced as she walked around the picnic table to where Rose was still sitting. She couldn't comprehend what was happening. This was crazy. Was she finally going to find out who The Midnight Flower was?

"Come on, I'll drive us to his house," Reggie offered, heading toward downtown, where he must have parked his car.

Rose followed him. Holly walked behind her, probably keeping an eye on Rose and making sure she didn't try to run. The thought crossed her mind, but only briefly. This was important. It was monumental. She had been dying to find out The Midnight Flower's true identity all summer.

She entertained the idea of calling someone to let them know she was going to an undisclosed location with Holly and Reggie. However, besides calling the police, which seemed like a terrible idea, or her parents, who would only talk her out of it, she was out of options. Her list of connections shrank with every passing day. That was the reason she had asked for help from her two exes. Apparently, their hatred ran deeper than she initially thought.

When they reached Reggie's red pick-up truck, Reggie dug around behind the driver's seat and thrust an old T-shirt into her face.

Rose crinkled her nose at the smell of sweat and BO. "What's that?"

"We can't let you find out where we're going," Holly explained with a small shrug. "You'll have to be blindfolded, so you can't lead the police back to The Midnight Flower's lair."

"His *lair*?" Rose squeaked out.

This sounded more and more like a Marvel movie. Was she letting the villain's lackeys lead her right into his trap?

Reggie chuckled and ran a hand through his slicked-back dark hair. "It really is like a lair. He hardly leaves that place ever since—" Reggie clapped a hand over his own mouth and stopped talking.

Holly narrowed her eyes at Reggie. "Since what? Are you hiding something from me?"

"What are you talking about?" Rose asked, holding the T-shirt in her hands.

"Nothing, never mind," Reggie said, shaking his head.

"Here. I'll help you." Holly took the T-shirt from Rose and tied it around her head. She led Rose into the truck, buckled her seatbelt, and sat down next to her.

"I'm glad you care so much about my safety," Rose mumbled sarcastically.

Holly rubbed her arm, and Rose felt goosebumps prickle across her skin from where her ex-girlfriend touched her. Holly leaned close to Rose to whisper in her ear, "The Midnight Flower won't hurt you. This is all part of the plan."

"But why?" Rose whispered back.

She heard the engine of the truck rev up and assumed Reggie had turned the key in the ignition. The truck rumbled to life, and she felt whiplash as they drove through town—well, she assumed so, at least. She truly had no clue where they were headed.

There was silence for the rest of the car ride. Holly didn't speak another word until the truck came to an abrupt stop.

"Come on, let's go." Holly gripped her by the elbow and pulled her out of the car.

When she was standing on the concrete, another hand gripped her other side. She assumed it was Reggie. They led her forward, directing her so she didn't run into anything or trip.

Shortly after, Rose heard a doorbell ringing. The door opened, and a man's voice greeted them. His voice didn't sound familiar, so she was still puzzled about the situation.

"Reggie. Holly," the man said, and after a slight pause, he added, "Rose."

Rose swallowed hard and let Reggie and Holly lead her inside of what she assumed was the man's house. Holly's soft hand helped her get situated on what felt like a couch, and then she untied the blindfold, letting her see again at last.

Rose was right. She was sitting on a leather couch in between Holly and Reggie. Across from them were two chairs. In one sat a man who appeared oddly familiar, but she couldn't quite place him.

But when Rose's gaze turned to the tiny figure in the second chair, her heart stuttered and nearly stopped beating. Waves of shock radiated throughout her body. Rose wanted to cry, throw up, scream, or any combination of those three actions.

Next to the man was a skinny redhead with wide green eyes and freckles—her sister. Rose rushed forward, pulling her sister into a tight embrace, stroking her hair and crying.

"Lily!"

Chapter 53: Rose

Her sister was alive. Elation filled Rose like the warming sensation of the first sip of hot chocolate on a cool evening.

Lily wasn't dead—it seemed too good to be true.

Lily hugged her back, laughing and crying at the same time. "I'm so happy to see you," Lily said, clinging to her.

"Me too. I never gave up. Neither did Mom and Dad. We never stopped looking for you." Rose stepped back from Lily to examine her more closely. She wiped tears from her eyes. "Are you okay? Have you been here this whole time? Where are we?"

She calculated how long they had been driving. They had to be near Spartanburg or still in town. The drive hadn't been very long. Maybe ten minutes. Had Lily been so close to them this whole time?

"I'm f-fine, Rose," Lily stuttered.

She immediately knew her sister was lying. She couldn't see any discernible bruises or marks that proved she had been tortured, but that didn't mean much. She had been missing for a year, presumed dead, so it couldn't have been a happy year. Her sister wasn't stupid. She would have escaped if there was a way out.

Rose heard a startled yelp come from the other side of the room, where

Holly stood beside Reggie. Reggie stumbled. Holly must have pushed him, but Rose had been focused on her sister, so she missed it.

"This is what you meant, isn't it, Reggie? You knew Lily was here this entire time, and you didn't try to save her? What the hell is wrong with you?" Holly said, rage settling on her pretty face.

Reggie narrowed his eyes. "I thought you knew too."

"I just found out a month ago! I had to wait for the right moment to come back. You've known for months and didn't try to help her?" Holly said.

"It's not what you think. It's not creepy. He loves her!" Reggie sputtered, attempting to justify his actions.

Holly glared at him. "Are you kidding me? You can't think this is okay. You can't. Unless you feel the same . . ." Holly's voice dropped even lower. "Have you been spending time with Lily too?"

Reggie grumbled a response, but Rose didn't care about her exes bickering. She didn't know whom to believe anymore.

Rose squinted at the man. She held Lily's hand, vowing to protect her sister no matter what. She would get them both home safely. "Who are you?"

The man chuckled and went to the kitchen counter, grabbing a pair of glasses. He put them on and ran a hand through his hair, messing it up a bit. "Ring any bells? I must say, I'm hurt you don't remember me. It wasn't that long ago that I was your English teacher, Rose."

Her mind flashed back to a year ago, and she realized who he must be. Although, he looked different—skinnier, his hair was much lighter and longer, and—was he wearing contacts to change his eye color?

"Mr. Mortensen?" she asked.

He slowly clapped in a mocking gesture and smiled sardonically at her. "Very good, Rose! A plus for my former star pupil. Although I'm afraid I wasn't a very good teacher if it took you a year to find your sister. I expected you here months ago. I guess I didn't teach you enough. Or was the problem that you didn't pay close enough attention?"

Rose opened her mouth with a retort, but he held up a finger, silencing her.

"No, now isn't your turn to speak. You never read the book I gave you, did you? You never called me during the winter break of your freshman year. I waited and waited for you to text me, call me—*anything*! I gave you a precious gift. What did you do with it? Did you even open it?" Mr. Mortensen said, spittle flying from his mouth as his face reddened.

"I—I didn't realize how important it was to you. I'm sorry. I read it and I enjoyed it. But I didn't think it was appropriate for me to text or exchange numbers with a teacher," Rose lied, confused about what was happening.

She had completely forgotten about it. *Is this really all about a book?*

Mr. Mortensen laughed darkly and jerked his chin toward Lily. "Well, your sister didn't have that problem. When I failed to win you over, I transferred to the middle school. I wanted someone younger, more . . . pliable. I scouted out my next perfect flower, and I found Lily. After I learned she was your younger sister, it made the game even sweeter. I gave her gifts and won her heart. I waited for her to make the first move. Eventually, she asked for my phone number so we could talk. She was lonely and soaked up the attention." His eyes pinned on Lily like a predator on its prey. "I picked the wrong sister the first time, but I learned my lesson. Lily was the right choice all along."

He came over to them and pulled Lily's hand away from Rose, instead taking it in his own and kissing it tenderly. He tucked a few errant hairs behind Lily's ear. Lily's face flushed, and at first, Rose thought it was from Mr. Mortensen touching her—gross. But then Lily yanked her hand from his and moved closer to Rose.

Rose's stomach roiled, and she held her hand to it, willing it to calm down.

Oh God . . . Lily has been trapped here with this monster for a year. Who knows what he's done to her? This is all my fault.

The wheels spun in her head as she pieced together this newfound information with what she had already discovered. It was twisted and sickening, and she was absolutely furious. Rose couldn't bear to think about what her sister had endured for the past year. But more importantly, she had to focus on getting them out of there.

"Why don't you sit back down, Rose?" Mr. Mortensen waved a hand toward the couch. He put his hand on the small of Lily's back and guided her to the chair she had been sitting in previously. He remained standing, probably wanting to tower over them, the only one in a position of power.

"All right. Then I want an explanation." Rose sat on the couch again and folded her hands in her lap, so she didn't clench them into fists and punch the sicko who had kidnapped her sister. She wanted to do a lot more than punch him.

No one spoke. Rose assumed her initial fear that this was a trap was correct. How would she get herself and her sister home safely?

"Where's Spencer?" she asked, hoping someone would answer at least one of her questions.

Lily glanced toward the hallway, so Rose focused her attention on her.

"Is he here, Lily? Is he okay?" Rose asked.

Spencer came out of the shadows, brandishing a gun. Rose raced over to him, caressing his face and kissing him repeatedly. That is, until she noticed how distant he seemed.

"Spence? Are you all right?" she asked, her voice wavering.

"Sit down!" Spencer yelled, pointing the gun at her.

"Spencer, what are you doing?"

"Sit the fuck down," he screamed.

"Okay, okay. There's no need for the gun. I'll sit down." Rose obeyed him and sat, her heart now pounding in her chest with fear. This was her worst nightmare.

Mr. Mortensen, Holly, Reggie, and now Spencer... Lily was the only one in the room on her side, and even that was iffy. She had been held captive—who knew what her mental state was like? After being trapped in this prison for so long, Lily might not have a good grip on reality. Rose couldn't count on anyone but herself.

"Will someone please tell me what's going on?" Rose begged, putting her head in her hands as she sank into the leather couch once again.

The sting of betrayal struck Rose deeply. Not only had Spencer betrayed her, but he had known where Lily was. The only question was... had he known the entire time? Rose couldn't believe he would put Lily in danger like that. He had always treated her as a younger sister. So, why hadn't he told her as soon as he knew Lily was alive? He knew how much her sister's disappearance had affected her, not to mention their parents. Why would he hide that from them?

Reggie piped up first. "You know what you did to us, Rose." He pointed to his chest, then to Holly, Mr. Mortensen, and Spencer. "You used all of us and then broke up with us when you found your next victim. You're the only girl who ever treated me that way, and I still can't understand why!"

Mr. Mortensen chimed in next. "He's right. You did this to yourself, Rose. You thought you could flirt with everyone, tease and seduce us all, make us fall in love with you, then throw us away like used-up tissues when you were done with us. You can't treat people that way and get away with it. *You just can't,*" he growled.

"What are you talking about? I didn't do that to all of you. And I'm still dating Spencer, so he doesn't fit into that scenario," Rose argued.

"You always flirted with me!" Mr. Mortensen exploded. "Teasing me with your low-cut shirts and your high-pitched, nervous giggles. Finding excuses to be alone with me in my classroom. You wanted me, but you never followed through."

"B-but we—" Rose started.

"It was one kiss, Rose, and it wasn't nearly enough. I wanted so much more from you." His eyes roamed hungrily over her body, making Rose regret her V-neck blouse and tight pants.

"What?" This was Lily's turn to explode. "You kissed her?" She pointed an accusatory finger at Mr. Mortensen.

"Um, yes, my flower, but it was months before you and I were together. I promise. I never betrayed you," Mr. Mortensen fumbled to explain.

"But I thought you loved me." Lily clenched her hands into fists at her sides as she stood and paced the room.

Mr. Mortensen pulled Lily, who was now sobbing hysterically, into his arms. He tilted her chin up, so she was staring at him. "I love you, Lily, which is why we have to get rid of your sister. Rose has always been a nuisance. Now that she knows who I am, she won't rest until I'm locked away in prison for the rest of my life. You don't want that, do you? We'll never be able to see each other again or be together. We won't get our happily ever after that we've dreamed of. In five more years, you'll be eighteen and we can get married. Then we can have a family of our own someday. Imagine it, Lily, a perfect family that we create together."

Lily's bottom lip trembled. Rose hoped she wouldn't give in to this madness, but she didn't know what her sister was capable of. She didn't know Lily at all anymore. This person in front of her was entirely different from her timid twelve-year-old sister, her little sister who used to have a crush on Spencer and had never kissed a boy. So much had changed since then. For the worse.

Rose knew she had to intervene. "Lily, please don't listen to him. He's brainwashed you into being with him and tried to convince you he loves you, but he doesn't. He's an adult, and he's been taking advantage of you. I don't know what he's made you do . . ." She didn't want to dwell on what her sister had potentially endured at the hands of a grown man. "But it doesn't matter. I love you. Mom and Dad love you. We all want you to come home to be with us as a family again. Please don't believe a word he says. He wants to get rid of me because he knows I'm right. What he's doing is wrong, and he's made you believe him over the people who truly care about you. Mr. Mortensen isn't your family. I am."

Lily hesitated and then turned toward her, her green eyes watery-looking, as if she was about to cry. "Why didn't you find me? Didn't you miss me? Why would I want to go home and be judged by everyone for my choices? Everyone will find out what happened to me."

Rose took a step toward her sister, but Mr. Mortensen jerked Lily behind him, hiding her from view. "Lily, that isn't true. I thought about you every single day. I didn't know how much I could miss you until you were gone. I have so many regrets, but most of all, I regret the time we lost together and how I treated you in the days leading up to your disappearance. I should have been a better sister. If I was the older sister you deserved, you never would have ended up here, and I hope someday you can forgive me. All I want is for us to start over and strengthen our relationship. I want my sister back. I love you, Lily."

Lily shoved Mr. Mortensen away from her and stepped away from him. "Rose, run!"

Chapter 54: Rose

Rose grabbed Lily's arm, shielding her sister's body with her own. She didn't know what Mr. Mortensen or any of his little lackeys were going to do. She couldn't trust Spencer anymore, as he had been standing in the hallway holding a gun throughout their conversation and not speaking. Did that mean he was on Mr. Mortensen's side? Had he truly betrayed her?

Rose lifted her chin defiantly and stared at Mr. Mortensen, who had stumbled after Lily pushed him. He was back on his feet and glaring down at her.

"You're going to let us out of here," Rose told him. "My sister gave you part of herself that she shouldn't have had to lose, and that's on you. I don't know what you've told her all this time, but she should be at home with me and our parents, not locked away in a house with a pedophile."

Lily held her hand to her mouth and began biting her nails.

Mr. Mortensen sneered at Rose. "Who do you think you are, coming into my house and telling me what to do? You don't get to make the rules, Rose. Don't you realize that by now?" He pointed at Holly, Reggie, and Spencer. "When I approached each of your exes, it wasn't hard to convince them to help me. It didn't take much nudging after you destroyed each of their hearts. And Spencer, he was the easiest one of all." Mr. Mortensen snickered as he yanked Lily toward him and wrapped his arms around her. "Lily is mine, but you're free to leave if you wish. If you truly believe I'm a monster holding her captive or whatever nonsense is floating around your head, wouldn't you want to stay here to make sure she's safe?"

"St-stay here?" Rose stuttered, staring up at her former teacher.

Mr. Mortensen smiled brilliantly, a smile Rose had once seen as charming, but she now found it repulsive. "Yes, the idea just came to me. I don't know why I didn't think of it sooner, but it's marvelous. The more I think about it, the more I think I might have had the wrong idea before. I was so set on getting revenge against you for how you treated me . . . I went after your sister. I chose her because she was special. Unique. And pretty, of course. She looks so much like you. I've always preferred redheads." He smiled, exposing his teeth like a wolf to their prey just before striking and tearing into their flesh. "But maybe . . . Maybe you can stay here too." He held one of Lily's hands and held out the other hand to Rose. "The three of us can live here together. There's enough of me for both of you. I think as sisters you already know how to share."

Rose stared at his hand, unblinking, barely comprehending what he was suggesting. "Are you asking if I'll stay here with you and you'll . . . what exactly?" she asked in disbelief, unable to finish the sentence

"Well, Rose, I would consider you both my girlfriends. My *two* perfect flowers," Mr. Mortensen said with a feverish lust in his eyes.

Spencer stepped further into the room and came toward them. Rose wasn't sure if he was going to hurt her or save her. She figured it could go either way at this point, considering most of the people she loved had betrayed her. What had she done so horribly wrong to deserve this?

Mr. Mortensen let his hand fall back to his side and dug around in the pocket of his nerdy cardigan for a moment before pulling out a small handgun. "Spencer, don't you dare come any closer."

Spencer took another step forward. "Let them go, James," he said through gritted teeth.

"Why should I?" Mr. Mortensen raised an eyebrow.

Holly spoke up. "Because . . . because they don't deserve this. No one does."

Reggie stared at Holly, his eyes narrowing to slits. "Holly, what are you doing? Don't you remember what Rose did to us? She needs to pay for what she did!"

Holly stood from her position on the couch and came to stand beside Spencer. "Of course I remember all the pain, the hurt, and heartbreak. But you know what else I remember? The laughter, the fun times, the memories with her I'll never forget." She smiled sadly, her gaze becoming almost shy as she dropped her eyes to the ground. After a moment of silence, she spoke again. "What's more important is that, as humans, we have to learn how to forgive and move on from the past. We can't cling to our memories and our pain. Forgiveness makes us stronger."

Rose felt tears fall down her cheeks and brushed them away roughly.

"Let them go," Spencer repeated.

Reggie jumped up from the couch in a fast motion, tackling Spencer to the ground and wrestling the gun from his hand. Spencer was average in size, a guy who spent his free time reading comics and playing video games, so he didn't stand a chance against Reggie's muscular physique. With the gun in his hand, Reggie stood next to Mr. Mortensen, back to back.

Spencer groaned and got to his feet. He held out his hands toward them as he moved closer to Rose and Lily. "Please, can we talk this out? There must be some sort of agreement we can reach."

That sounded crazy, but Rose knew he must be trying to appease Mr. Mortensen so he would let them go. Spencer was going to save them. They would be okay. They would all get out of this alive.

"No. I don't like repeating myself, so I won't. I already gave them my best offer. It's a great opportunity that they would be stupid to refuse." Mr. Mortensen turned to face Rose and Lily directly. "My perfect flowers, do you want to hear the alternative if you don't comply?"

Rose and Lily exchanged glances. Lily grabbed her hand and held it tightly. Rose wouldn't let go, not this time. No force on earth would let her leave this house without her sister.

"What?" Rose asked, sounding braver than she felt. She had to be strong. She had to save Lily.

If she brought her sister home, her parents would hopefully forgive her for how badly she had screwed up . . .

Mr. Mortensen stroked his chin with the gun, putting it on full display. It was a dumb, macho move. "If you refuse my offer, I'll keep you as my pets." His dark eyes flashed with a warning. "You'll have to do whatever I say, or you'll be punished. Lily had a taste of that when she didn't obey my wishes, so maybe she'll tell you. Staying with me willingly is your only option."

Lily sobbed and turned to Rose, burying her face in her chest and clutching Rose's shirt as she cried. She clung to her like she used to when they were little. Back when they were best friends. "Rose, we have to get out of here. We can't stay." Lily wiped her nose across her sleeve.

Rose's heart twisted with emotion. "Don't worry. We won't stay here, Lily. This is abuse. He tried to convince you it's normal, but it isn't. He's an adult, and he's tried to make you think his sick fetish is okay. I think you went along with it to survive. I understand. You didn't have a choice, but now you do." She squeezed her sister's hand again. "We both do. We're going home."

Reggie sneered at them and held the gun out, pointing it at Rose. "Bitch, you never had a choice." He jerked his head toward Mr. Mortensen. "James doesn't want you anymore. He only wants Lily. Leave or pay the consequences."

"I'm not leaving without her," Rose said in a firm voice.

Reggie cocked the gun, and his finger hovered over the trigger. "This is your last warning. If you don't leave, I'm going to kill you."

But Rose knew it wasn't that simple. She knew too much—and Lily knew even more. There was no way they would let them leave. They needed to escape before Reggie lost control and fired the gun.

Mr. Mortensen waved his hands around. "Now, now. Let's not make any hasty decisions. No one needs to die here. That wasn't part of my plan," he muttered.

Reggie's steely gaze turned on Mr. Mortensen. "You don't get to tell me what to do anymore. I brought her here. I did what you asked, but I'm acting without a script from here on out. Rose is a bitch, and she doesn't deserve your pathetic offer. She doesn't deserve to live."

The next few moments happened in slow motion. Spencer dove in front of Rose and Lily in a protective gesture, as Reggie pulled the trigger on the gun. The bullet tore through Spencer's chest, and he screamed a strangled cry, falling to the ground at Rose's feet.

Chapter 55: Rose

Rose kneeled onto the ground holding Spencer's head in her hands. "Spencer . . ." She sobbed as tears fell from her eyes and landed on his body.

"Did he hurt you? Are you okay?" Spencer asked in a strained voice, his eyes fluttering closed.

"I'm fine, but we need to get you to a hospital," Rose told him. "I promise you're going to make it."

Rose tried to help Spencer get back on his feet, but he was in immense pain and not much help. Lily wrapped one of Spencer's arms around her shoulder.

"Thanks," Rose said with a grateful nod to her sister.

Lily nodded back.

"Let's get out of here," Rose said.

Mr. Mortensen stepped forward, blocking their path. "*Uh, uh, uh* . . . you three aren't going anywhere. I'm disappointed in you, Spencer. You were my greatest asset. Although I wish Reggie hadn't shot you so recklessly . . . That's not what I would have chosen for your punishment of betraying me."

So many things made sense now. Ever since the first note from The

Midnight Flower, Rose had wondered how he knew so much about her. It had almost seemed like he had cameras in her house or her room was miked. But the horrible truth was that Spencer must have been feeding him information this whole time . . . That's how he knew her deepest, darkest secrets. Spencer had told him everything and used it against her to manipulate her.

An icy coldness washed over her at the full realization of her best friend's betrayal. She didn't know if she could forgive him. She couldn't make herself respond. It was too much.

Spencer held his hand to his chest. Blood soaked his shirt, seeping in between his fingers and dripping onto the fake hardwood floor, droplets splattering around them. "I didn't betray you. I was never on your side to begin with. I only did it to protect Rose. I figured it was better if I was the inside man, instead of someone else who didn't care about her."

Rose nearly let Spencer drop back onto the floor at his admission. "So, it's true, then? You've been working for him this whole time."

Spencer winced. "I'm sorry, Rose. It all started this summer. I didn't have a choice. It was the best way to help you. I thought I would find out more information about The Midnight Flower. I thought he was some harmless guy messing with you. Then he started taking it too far, and you were so scared . . . I wanted to tell you, but I couldn't. He said he would frame me for all of it. Until earlier today, I didn't know he was our old English teacher, or that this was all connected to Lily. He always wore a mask when we met. I swear, I didn't know he was involved with her. If I had known he had Lily—"

Rose barked a laugh, this time letting go of Spencer and standing, blood dripping down her legs from holding him. "What would you have done differently? Because you never cared about me to begin with. I don't trust a single word you've said."

She strode purposefully toward her sister and linked arms with her. "Lily, we're leaving. For real this time."

Mr. Mortensen moved to stand in front of the entryway, blocking their path to freedom. "No, my perfect flowers, I already told you. Why is it that you silly girls never listen? You aren't leaving. I gave you another option, but I was simply being polite. I want Lily. She's mine."

Reggie walked over to Mr. Mortensen and stood next to him. They each held a gun, although Mr. Mortensen aimed at the ground while Reggie pointed his gun toward Rose and Lily.

Mr. Mortensen sighed and yanked Reggie's arm down. "Reggie, we don't want more casualties on our hands! That would defeat the entire purpose of the past year! I never harmed a hair on Lily's pretty little head. I'm certainly not going to jail for murder or being an accomplice to murder."

Reggie grumbled an incoherent reply under his breath but lowered his gun.

Meanwhile, Rose saw out of the corner of her eye that Holly had snuck forward toward the two men, unnoticed. Rose wondered with anxiety and a little bit of hope whether Holly was going to help her and Lily escape. Hope was all she had left. Without hope, she had nothing.

Mr. Mortensen spoke up again. "Now we have to figure out what to do about Spencer." He eyed Spencer lying on the ground with more blood leaking out of his chest. "I'll have to clean the floors." He paused, then said in a dramatic voice, "That's a lot of blood. I think I'll need a bigger mop." He threw back his head and laughed sarcastically.

"*Nightmare on Elm Street*," Spencer said in a hoarse voice, emitting a sound that was somewhere between a laugh and a cough.

Mr. Mortensen pointed the gun at him. "Very good, Spencer. See? This is why I always liked you. You were an outstanding student. You know all about the classic horror movies." He shook his head in disappointment. "It's a shame I'll have to pin this on you. I'll tell the police how I heroically rescued Rose and Lily and killed you in a shootout. Yes . . . Yes, I think that will do nicely. I suppose I'll have to move again and find someone new, though. What a shame it didn't work out this time. Ah, well. There will always be pretty young girls wherever I move." The gun hung loosely from his hands.

Just then, Holly jumped forward, climbing onto Mr. Mortensen's back and covering his eyes with her hands. Rose attacked Reggie, hoping she could distract him, giving her sister an opening.

Lily snatched the gun from Reggie. "Get out of the way, Holly!" Lily warned.

Holly smoothly slid onto the ground and away from the door.

Everyone stared in shock as, in one fluid movement, Lily cocked the gun, faced Mr. Mortensen, and fired.

Chapter 56: Rose

Lily fired the gun again. This time, Mr. Mortensen slunk to the ground.

Holly turned to Rose. "What are you waiting for? Take Lily and get out of here!"

"B-but . . . what about Spencer?" Rose asked.

"Don't worry about him. I'll take him to the hospital," Holly said.

Rose wasn't sure if she believed her, but she didn't know what else to do. She took a deep breath, doing her best in the difficult situation to clear her head. Releasing the breath slowly, she calmed herself for the time being. She could do this. She could save her sister and Spencer. He had risked his life for them—to save them—so it was the least she could do for him. Even if he had betrayed her . . .

But she couldn't leave his fate to chance.

"I don't know where we are, and you brought me here," Rose pointed out.

"Right." Holly searched the room, her eyes landing on a row of hooks on the wall. She picked up the keys to a Subaru Outback and tossed them to Rose. "Here, take Mr. Mortensen's keys. I don't think he'll need them anymore. Now, go!"

Without thinking about it further, Rose ignored Holly's promise about taking Spencer to the hospital. She motioned for Lily to help her support Spencer while walking to the garage. She quickly unlocked the car, helped Lily settle Spencer into the backseat, and showed her how to apply pressure on his wound, then she clambered into the driver's seat.

As she pressed the garage door opener and the garage door slowly lifted, the door to the house opened and slammed. Reggie came out looking absolutely furious.

"You aren't going anywhere!" he screamed, slamming his fists down on the hood of the car.

Rose locked the car, put it into reverse, and sped out of the garage. After checking the back-up camera, she zoomed down the driveway, whipped around, and set off down the street.

She turned to meet her sister's eyes in the rearview mirror. "Do you know where we are?"

Lily nodded weakly. "Yeah, the neighborhood down the street from ours. Across the main road."

"Okay, then if I leave the neighborhood and follow the main road, I'll reach the highway. I can follow the signs for the hospital once I'm on the highway." Rose focused on driving for a moment before she added, "I can't believe you were so close to home this whole time. Just down the road, really, but we didn't know."

Lily sniffled in the backseat. "I know." She sighed deeply. "I was stupid. I shouldn't have trusted him. You never would have fallen for his lies like I did."

"It isn't your fault, Lily," she said fiercely. "He shouldn't have done any of this. He abused his position as your teacher—and mine."

"What are we going to tell Mom and Dad?" Lily wiped her nose on her sleeve as she cried harder.

"We'll tell them the truth. But don't worry about that. First, we need to get Spencer to the hospital."

Rose drove over the speed limit the entire way to the hospital, not caring about potentially getting a speeding ticket or the consequences of reckless driving. The three of them had been through so much trauma that she didn't think anything would faze them ever again.

They arrived at the hospital fifteen minutes later. Instead of parking the car, Rose turned on the hazards and left the car in front of the hospital entrance. If anyone knew their circumstances, they wouldn't protest her illegal parking. Besides, the car was registered in Mr. Mortensen's name, anyway.

Rose went around to the backseat to wait with Spencer. She ordered Lily to find a wheelchair and get help.

As Rose stood beside her former best friend and boyfriend, he said her name softly.

"Rose."

"Yeah, Spence?" she said automatically, the familiar nickname tumbling out of her mouth without conscious thought.

"Am I going to be okay?" He stared up at her, his normally vibrant hazel eyes dull.

"Of course. You'll be fine." She squeezed his hand.

When Rose was about to utter more reassurances, Lily came running out of the hospital with a toned orderly pushing a wheelchair behind her.

"He's right here!" Lily said, out of breath. She bent at the waist, holding her hands on her knees.

The orderly easily lifted Spencer into the wheelchair. "I'll get him in to see a doctor. Are either of you family?" He glanced between Rose and Lily.

"No, we're his friends. We know his mom, though. Should we call her?" Rose said.

"Yes, and tell her to bring his insurance information and an ID," the orderly said in a calm voice, pushing Spencer toward the hospital entrance.

"Okay, I can do that." Rose pulled out her phone to call Spencer's mom.

Before she could scroll through her contacts, the orderly continued his line of questioning.

"How did this happen?" The orderly peered at them curiously as Rose and Lily followed him into the hospital.

"Um, it's kind of a long story . . ." Rose started.

Chapter 57: Rose

Rose and Lily were back at home, safe and sound, with their parents in their family room. Rose had called Fiona, Spencer's mom, and she had rushed to the hospital. Then she called her own parents, who had already been on their way there after Fiona relayed the news about Spencer. Rose had only told them the minimal details, but to say her parents were shocked and overjoyed to reunite with their missing daughter after a year would be an understatement. The Blackwood family had shared a tearful, bittersweet reunion.

Fiona remained at the hospital waiting for news about Spencer. The doctors hadn't provided an update, and no one knew if Spencer would make it yet.

The guilt threatened to overwhelm Rose because it was her fault Spencer was in this mess. It was her fault he had worked for The Midnight Flower and double-crossed him. Her fault he had tried saving her and taken the bullet meant for her. Her fault if he died . . .

"Rose? Rose, are you okay?" her sister asked, shaking her shoulder.

Rose drifted back to the present—to her awful reality, where she and Lily had the terrible task of telling their parents what happened. They had agreed—no more lies, but that didn't make it any easier.

Lily relayed her horrific tale of the past year, skimming over her day-to-day life and romantic relationship with Mr. Mortensen. Lily might not be ready to talk about all of it, but she would need to share the details with someone eventually. It couldn't be healthy to keep it all bottled up inside. A therapist would be better qualified to help her. Lily would have a lot of emotions to sort through.

Either way, Lily was brave as she told her family the story. Rose looked at her fondly, so relieved her little sister was home at last. She still couldn't believe she had been so close to their house this entire time, and no one had known. Why had no one suspected Mr. Mortensen? Had he done such a stellar job of hiding his relationship with Lily? Rose didn't see how it was possible. Surely, someone had known . . . But if Rose and her parents didn't know, then who else was there?

Her mom sobbed throughout Lily's story, while her dad's face darkened more than she thought physically possible.

At the end, Lily said, "Then Spencer jumped in front of us, and the bullet hit him right in the chest. Holly helped us leave. Rose took the car keys to James's Subaru"—Rose and her parents all cringed at Lily's casual use of Mr. Mortensen's first name—"and she drove us to the hospital." Lily's eyes shined with tears. "I didn't have time to tell you earlier, but thank you, Rose. Thank you for staying there to make sure I got out. I don't know what would have happened if you had left me there with him and his . . . gang, or whatever they are." Lily shivered delicately.

Her mom moved closer to Lily. "Do you need a sweater? Or I can adjust the thermostat? Is it too cold in here?" She peered earnestly at Lily. "I think we have some hot cocoa in the pantry too." She moved toward the kitchen, but Lily stopped her with a hug.

"Mom, I'm fine, I swear. Just a little freaked out still," Lily said.

"I wouldn't blame you if you were absolutely terrified after what you've been through," her dad said. "This will be a change for you, but you have the rest of the summer to get used to being home again and living a normal life. I'll call some of my connections on Monday and hire a lawyer. The police told me that Mr. Mortensen escaped. He must have fled the scene after you two left."

Rose shook her head. "There's no way he survived. Lily shot him twice. He must be dead."

"Ha, that's my girl!" her dad said. "If he ever shows his face in this town again, I'll shoot him myself. The sick freak."

"Please, stop!" Lily screamed, sounding hysterical.

Lily shoved her mom's arms away and sprinted up the stairs, presumably to her bedroom. A door slammed, and soon, loud pop music came from her speakers.

Rose's parents both turned to look at her, stunned.

"This will be difficult for all of us, but for Lily, especially. But we have to ask you, Rose . . . Did you ever suspect Mr. Mortensen of doing this?" her mom asked, clenching her dad's hand as she sat next to him on the loveseat.

***

Freshman year – November

Rose giggled, and a blush spread across her cheeks. "Thanks, Mr. Mortensen." She took the dark red rose from him and sniffed it, inhaling the scent deeply until it filled up her nostrils.

"You're welcome, my perfect flower." He smiled at her and brushed his hand against her cheek, leaning in closer and closer.

She gasped at his touch on her skin. It felt like her cheek was on fire, and she was melting under his fingers. No one had ever made her feel this way. Not even Holly. He was the reason Rose had broken up with her.

Mr. Mortensen's hand drifted down her neck to her collarbone, tracing lines down her chest. She felt the fire building within her and thought she would explode with the feeling as he moved in impossibly close, crushing his lips against hers in a moment of passion. No one had ever kissed her like this. She kissed him back, becoming lightheaded with the heated kissing.

The bell rang in the hallway, signaling the end of the lunch period. The moment between them shattered, and Rose came back to reality with a sickening sensation in her stomach. What was she doing? She was in Mr. Mortensen's classroom—her English teacher, for Pete's sake!—and they were making out. Why had she let him touch her and kiss her? Yeah, he was hot, but wasn't it wrong? She was his student, and she had just turned fourteen and a half. Wasn't that creepy?

Rose tried to tell herself it was okay and to lose herself in the moment again, but she couldn't this time. All she could think about were the consequences. She couldn't let this go on any longer. What if he started wanting more from her?

When he broke away, Rose gasped. "Mr. Mortensen," she muttered softly.

"Yes, Rose?" he said, his voice sounding deep and sexy.

"I—I need to get to class," she said, squirming out of his tight embrace.

Mr. Mortensen chuckled and kissed her again, smacking her butt as she turned to grab her backpack. "Okay, don't be late for your next class. See you tomorrow," he said, his eyes glimmering with lust.

***

Present day

Should she be honest with her parents and tell them what had really happened? How Mr. Mortensen had gone after her first, and when she refused him after some flirting and one stupid kiss, he had gone for Lily?

Rose regretted the kiss and how he had tricked her into thinking she was special, that she was the exception to the rule. Now she could plainly see he must have done the same to other young girls until he found one who would give in to him. With a shudder, she realized it was just as likely that she could have been kidnapped and held hostage as her sister was.

Rose pretended to inspect the ground, sliding her socked foot across the floor, stalling to answer. "Yeah, I knew he was interested in other female students at school, but I didn't know he would take it this far. If I had known, I would have spoken up sooner. If I had thought he kidnapped Lily, I swear I would have told you. I never suspected he was involved in this."

"Okay, we believe you, sweetie. Thank you for telling us. We'll get this whole Midnight Flower mess sorted out," her dad promised, squeezing her arm. "If what you said is true and Mr. Mortensen is dead, then the worst is behind us. There's nothing to worry about. You and Lily are both safe. Finally, my two girls are back home."

Chapter 58: Rose

"Rose?" a soft voice called.

Rose sat up in bed, waking from her light sleep in a panic, scrambling to find her cell phone. She shone the light toward the figure standing in her doorway.

"Who is it?" she screeched, in a much quieter voice than she intended. Her words were garbled by her instantaneous fear.

"Lily?" she said as her phone illuminated the figure in the doorway and practically blinded her sister.

Lily protested and shielded her face with her hands. "It's me. Put that fricking light away."

"What's wrong? Are you okay?" Rose rolled out of bed and turned on the small lamp on her desk.

"Yeah, I'm fine. It's just—There's something I . . ." Lily sighed and took a deep breath, walking further into the room.

"What is it? Did you have a nightmare? Do you want to sleep in my room tonight?" Rose's tone softened, and she reached out to her sister in comfort. She didn't mind if Lily stayed in her room until she adjusted to being home again.

She couldn't imagine what Lily was going through. At least she was home safely, but she probably wouldn't be able to sleep normally for a while.

"Um, no. I'm sorry, Rose. I—" Lily said, but she stopped talking when a tall, dark silhouette joined her in the bedroom.

Mr. Mortensen stood next to Lily and bent down to kiss her on top of her head. "My perfect flower, I missed you so much."

Lily's face looked ghostly white in the dim lighting. She flinched when Mr. Mortensen touched her.

Rose balled her hands into fists at her sides. She backed away from them. "How did you get in our house? What the hell is going on?"

"You didn't think I would let you both get away, did you?" Mr. Mortensen asked as a sinister grin curled up his face. "I've been hiding out at Reggie's house all night. He drove me here. I want Lily, and I'm not letting her go this time."

Was that fear flickering in Lily's eyes? Surely, she didn't want to go back to captivity . . .

Rose backed up further until she was standing by the only window in her bedroom. "*This is Lily's home* with me and our parents. Not with you . . . you *monster*," she snarled.

Rose lifted the window seat compartment and pulled out a box containing a small handgun. Her dad had given it to her after the incident with the stalker showing up at their house. He didn't want her to be defenseless. She knew the gun was loaded, so she pointed it at Mr. Mortensen.

"Let go of Lily, and back away slowly," Rose commanded in a growl.

Mr. Mortensen chuckled and patted Lily's arm. "My perfect flower, it's time we get rid of your sister once and for all. Then we can be together at last. We'll move far away from here and start our life together."

Lily tried to extricate herself from his arms as she glared at him. "No! I don't want to be with you. When will you realize I was miserable being trapped in that house with you? I did what I had to so I could survive."

Rose barely had time to register that her sister didn't want to be with Mr. Mortensen before her bedroom door flung open. The sound of a shotgun being cocked tore through the night as an enormous figure loomed in the doorway.

"What the hell . . . Who's there?" Mr. Mortensen barked at the new addition.

The bedroom door shut, and the light flickered on, illuminating Rose and Lily's dad standing there in his pajamas, his green eyes flashing with anger at the intruder in their house.

Her dad lifted the gun, aiming at Mr. Mortensen. "Get the fuck away from my daughters, you creep!"

Mr. Mortensen responded by pulling Lily in front of him and wrapping his arms around her waist. "I don't think so. I'm not letting her out of my grasp that easily. Never again. If you shoot me, you'll have to shoot Lily too."

Lily's green eyes, identical to their dad's, shimmered with unshed tears. Rose couldn't let Lily leave with Mr. Mortensen. They needed to incapacitate him. Rose and her dad both had guns, but what did that matter if they accidentally shot Lily?

Rose made eye contact with her dad, hoping he had a plan. She was glad he was there, but she wondered what she could do. Hopefully something to make Mr. Mortensen let go of Lily and leave peacefully without harming her sister any further. *Well*, the thought entered her mind, *he wanted me first . . .*

Rose uncocked the gun and put the safety back on. She tossed the gun onto the bed and stepped toward Mr. Mortensen and Lily. "I have a proposition for you. Leave Lily here."

Mr. Mortensen opened his mouth to protest, but Rose continued speaking. "Leave Lily here at home, safe and sound, and take me with you instead."

Her dad yelled, "No!" and moved toward them. He grabbed Lily and held his younger daughter in his arms.

Lily sobbed, falling to her knees, despite her dad trying to hold her up. "No, please . . . Don't do this, James. Don't take my sister from me. I can't stand the thought of losing her when I'm finally home with my family again," she pleaded.

Mr. Mortensen smiled darkly. "I don't think so. I'm not interested in Rose any more. Lily is the one my soul craves." He turned to Lily, extending his hand to her. "Come on, Lily. No sense in waiting around for the police to show up. I'm sure your lovely father has already called them."

But her dad threw Lily onto the bed, out of harm's way, and rushed toward Mr. Mortensen, tackling him with a guttural grunt. Rose ran to her sister to make sure she was okay. Lily didn't appear physically harmed, but she sat on the bed sobbing quietly.

When Rose turned back to her dad and Mr. Mortensen, Mr. Mortensen had the upper hand. Her dad must have dropped the gun in the scuffle, and Mr. Mortensen was pummeling him in the face repeatedly. Her dad took the punches with only minimal winces, but it had to hurt like hell. His face was becoming a bloody mess.

"Lily, we have to stop him! He's hurting Dad. He's going to kill him if we don't interfere!" Rose warned her sister.

With a wild scream, Lily grabbed Rose's handgun, screaming. "You asshole. You can't have either of us. I hope you rot in hell!"

Rose wrestled the gun from her sister's hand, not wanting her to be the one to live with the guilt of murder. She sprinted forward and shot Mr. Mortensen in the forehead.

Mr. Mortensen fell to the ground and was dead within a matter of seconds. A pool of blood formed around his head. There was a gaping hole in his head where the bullet had entered.

"I-is he d-dead?" Lily stuttered, directing the question to her dad with wide, green eyes like a cat's.

Her dad groaned and crawled over to Mr. Mortensen's body, where he checked his wrist for a pulse. "Good aim, Rose. All those classes at the shooting range really paid off, huh?" he joked.

Lily snickered, then Rose did too. It was all they could do to handle the grim situation. Sometimes it was better to laugh in the face of death.

Chapter 59: Rose

Red and blue lights flashed through Rose's bedroom window. Only the tiniest bit of relief flickered through her at the sign of law enforcement. If they had arrived sooner, then she wouldn't have been forced to kill someone. Goosebumps prickled across every inch of her exposed skin. She shivered in her thin tank top and shorts. She had almost become a murder victim, or worse, Mr. Mortensen's next kidnapped girl.

Her dad pulled back the curtains to see outside. "Looks like the cops are here, finally. It's about damn time. That security system is supposed to have a rapid response to any trespassers. I'll stay in here with the body. You girls go downstairs and let the cops inside, okay?"

Rose dragged her sister toward the door. "Come on, Lily."

Lily shook her head, shaking free from Rose's grasp. "No! I want to stay here. With James."

"But . . . why?" Rose tilted her head to the side in concern.

The doorbell rang, and a fist pounded on the front door. "Police, open up! We received a 911 call!"

"Girls, go downstairs! Your mother is going to wake up. She'll be pissed at me if she thinks I knowingly put you in danger," her dad said. "Go. Now!"

The doorbell rang again. "Is anyone in the house? We're going to use force to enter!"

"I'm not going anywhere," Lily wailed. "I can't leave him." She lay over Mr. Mortensen's body, sobbing hysterically with her head on his chest.

Rose met her dad's eyes. He shrugged and with a deep sigh, said, "Okay, Rose, you go let them inside. Hurry before they break down the door."

Without another word, Rose bounded out of her room and down the stairs. She opened the front door to reveal multiple police officers and police cars parked in the driveway.

"Hello, miss," the shorter of the two officers said in a strong southern accent, tipping his hat at her. "We're answering a distress call from about twenty minutes ago. Are you okay?"

"Yes, I'm fine. The body is upstairs," Rose answered in a monotone voice. She rubbed her exposed arms as a breeze whipped through.

"The . . . *what*?" the taller police officer sputtered, gawking at Rose and trying to peer into the house. "What's your name, miss?"

"Rose Blackwood."

"I'm Officer Williams, and my partner here is Officer Ortega. Can we come inside? What happened here tonight?" the shorter police officer said.

"Um, well, it's kind of complicated. My dad and sister are upstairs . . . with a dead man."

"An intruder?" Officer Williams asked, raising an eyebrow. "Self-defense?"

"Something like that," Rose muttered, opening the door wider to let them in. "I'll show you upstairs."

As Rose led them up the staircase, her mom, wearing sweatpants and a faded T-shirt, came out of her bedroom and stood at the top of the stairs staring down at them. Her hand gripped the banister.

"Rose, what's going on?" she demanded in a shrill tone. "Where are your father and Lily?"

"They're fine, Mom. They're—" Rose began, but Officer Ortega cut her off.

"Rose, go into that bedroom with your mother until we come get you, okay? Can you do that?" Officer Ortega pointed to the main bedroom.

"Sure," Rose said, not wanting to cause any more trouble.

Her mom protested, "But what about my husband and my other daughter? Where are they?"

"This is a dangerous situation, ma'am, and we don't know all the details yet. We'll let you know as soon as we have the answers. Take your daughter in there and lock the door," Officer Ortega directed.

Her mom turned to Rose with tears trembling on her eyelashes. Rose took her mom's arm and guided her into the main bedroom. It was for their own safety. Besides, Lily and her dad were fine. Mr. Mortensen was dead, so nothing bad could happen to them.

Rose shut the bedroom door and turned the lock. She escorted her mom over to the bed and helped her sit down. Her mom seemed like a zombie, barely coherent or present, like she had acted back in the days when Lily first went missing. Rose hoped she would be okay after she told her what had happened.

"Mom, Mr. Mortensen broke into the house tonight. He was going to take—"

"He did *what*? Where is he now? I'll kill him!" Her mom sprang back to life at the mention of Lily's kidnapper.

"He's dead," Rose said bluntly, wincing at the expression on her mom's face. She quickly added, "But Dad and Lily are fine. They're in my bedroom with his body."

"How did this happen? We have a security alarm and cameras. How did he get past them without setting them off? We should have received an alert on our phones. The police are supposed to be notified immediately," her mom said. "We're going to switch security systems after this if it doesn't work properly. This is the exact reason we installed cameras and an alarm. I'm going to sue the security company!"

"Mom, I think Lily used the code to turn off the alarm. She must have disconnected the cameras too. She helped him get inside. That, or Reggie did it somehow."

"It must have been Reggie. My little Lily-pad wouldn't do that. She's a . . . a sweet girl. She never got into trouble before all this," her mom said.

"I know, but she's still confused. Lily's emotions are messed up." Rose sighed.

"Okay, well, let's not worry about that until we have some answers. We'll get to the bottom of this, so don't make any rash accusations against your sister."

Rose's initial reaction was to argue, but she didn't want to make the situation worse. Her mom was right about one detail—she should wait until they knew exactly what had happened tonight. It had all been a blur from the moment Lily entered her bedroom and woke her up.

The important thing was Mr. Mortensen was dead. The nightmare of the past year was over at last. Or so she thought.

Chapter 60: Rose

After the police left, Rose and Lily's parents insisted that both girls sleep in the main bedroom with them. Her dad blew up the air mattress for Rose and Lily to share. Rose didn't protest because she was admittedly still freaked out by the whole situation. Although Mr. Mortensen was dead, she didn't feel safe. She wasn't sure when she would sleep through the night again without the fear of someone coming for her.

The police had told Lily she would have to come to the police station later that week to recount the events of the past year. They also wanted to know if Mr. Mortensen had any accomplices. They told the police about Reggie, Kylar, and Mason. Holly had helped them escape, so they left her out of it. Even though Spencer had betrayed Rose, he had risked his life to save her, so Rose didn't want Lily to mention him as being involved in Mr. Mortensen's shenanigans. Plus, Spencer was still in the hospital. He was in critical condition, and the doctors didn't know if he would pull through. Rose planned to visit him the next morning—well, that same morning, considering it was after 3:00 a.m. She needed a few hours of sleep before facing that obstacle, though.

Curling up on the air mattress next to her sister, Rose tried to avoid moving much because every time she did, the air mattress made a squeaking sound that she was sure woke up her sister and parents. Although it wasn't the most comfortable, Rose was so exhausted that she eventually fell asleep.

After a while, Rose awoke to a squeak and her sister rolling off the air mattress. The room was still semi-dark, so it couldn't be that late in the morning yet. "Lily? Are you okay?"

Silently, Lily stalked toward the main bedroom door, reaching out for the doorknob. Rose slid off the air mattress to follow her out of the bedroom and downstairs. She quietly shut the bedroom door to let their parents rest more.

When Lily was in the kitchen rummaging around in the cupboards, she turned to Rose with a grimace. "Why did you follow me down here?"

"You didn't answer me when I asked if you're okay." She paused, eyeing her sister's tired eyes and pale skin warily. Rose knew she didn't look much better from the stress and lack of sleep. "So, are you?"

"*I'm fine*," Lily said through gritted teeth as she pulled out a box of cereal, then turned to the fridge to find the milk.

"Are you sure? Because I wouldn't blame you if you weren't. You've been through a lot," she said softly. She reached out to squeeze her sister's arm, but Lily moved out of reach, darting back to avoid her touch.

Rose retracted her hand and wrung her hands in front of her. "Lily, I'm so sorry. I promise I'll do my best to make it up to you. I—I know—"

"You don't know anything," Lily snarled at her. "You don't know what I've been through this past year. All you had to do was let me hang out with you and Spencer for an hour or two and then walk home with me. But you couldn't do the bare minimum for me. This is all your fault."

The harsh words stung, but her sister didn't mean it. She couldn't. She must still be processing her kidnapping and rescue. Rose had saved her life—that had to mean something, right?

Before Rose could muster a response, Lily added, "Just because your boyfriend betrayed you and put you in danger, then almost got you killed, that doesn't mean we're the same. I'm nothing like you."

A sharp pang went through her chest at the mention of Spencer. Rose was full of regret for what had happened to him, but more importantly, for not seeing the signs sooner that he was working for The Midnight Flower—Mr. Mortensen. If Rose had found out sooner, she could have stopped him or distanced herself from him before he revealed all her secrets.

Rose pressed her lips together. "Okay, well, I'm going back to bed. Will you be all right down here by yourself?"

Lily spooned more cereal into her mouth without replying, so Rose went upstairs and settled onto the air mattress, drifting into a restless sleep once again.

***

The second time she woke up, her parents were gone. Rose heard heated voices coming from downstairs. She knew the rest of her family must be awake, so she crept down the stairs to listen to their conversation.

"You don't understand me! You never have. That's why I left. I couldn't stand living in this house anymore. I was the good kid. I had straight A's, and I did everything right, but it wasn't enough. Rose was always getting into trouble, so you paid more attention to her. I had no one to turn to, no one who cared, so I got closer to James, and look what happened to me!" Lily screamed, presumably to their parents.

Rose heard sobbing and assumed that was coming from her mom.

"Lily, he's an adult, and you were his student. You understand why that type of relationship is wrong, don't you? You were only twelve when all this started. I wish you had talked to us and told us how you felt. We would have helped you," her dad said.

"I'm thirteen now, though. I'm old enough to make my own decisions," Lily countered.

Silence fell over the room. Rose took the opportunity to stroll leisurely into the kitchen, acting as if she hadn't overheard their conversation.

"Morning," she greeted her family.

They were all seated at the kitchen table, but when Rose came into the room, Lily stood from her seat and stalked off toward the stairs.

"Where are you going?" her dad called after her.

"To my room to get away from you," Lily retorted.

Rose sighed. "Give her space. Some alone time might be good for her to process everything."

Rose's phone rang. She quickly answered when she saw it was Fiona.

"Hello? Fiona?"

"Hi, Rose. I have an update about Spencer. I waited until I knew more, but Mr. Mortensen was listed as an organ donor, so they're doing an emergency surgery. Spencer might have a chance now," Fiona choked out in between sobs. "Can you come here? I don't want to be alone."

"Yes, of course. I'll be there soon."

Fiona ended the call. Rose stood in the kitchen, loosely gripping her phone in her hand, staring down at it and wondering if this was real.

"Is it okay if I go to the hospital to visit Spencer?" she asked her parents in a daze.

Her dad nodded, picking up the newspaper from where it lay folded on the table.

"Do you want me to go with you?" her mom asked.

"No, that's okay. I might be there for a while. Fiona said he's undergoing surgery right now. She doesn't want to be alone," Rose replied.

"All right. Please drive safely. Will you be home for dinner?" her mom asked.

"Yup. Love you both." Rose hugged each of her parents and left.

***

When Rose arrived at the hospital, she wandered around the waiting room until she spotted Fiona staring off blankly across the room.

"Fiona?" Rose said, approaching her with hesitation.

Fiona smiled weakly at her. "Hi, Rose. Thanks for coming."

"You're welcome. Is he . . . Is he going to be okay?"

Fiona's voice cracked as she answered. "The doctors said the bullet destroyed a lung and part of his heart. They're performing surgery on him, but when he arrived here, he had already lost so much blood. He was lucky enough to have an organ donor, but he needs a miracle to stand a fighting chance. I still have hope, though."

Rose sat in the chair next to her, wrapping her arm around Fiona's shoulders. "I'm so sorry," she told her. "This is all my fault. He did it to save me and Lily. He took the bullet that was meant for me."

Fiona smiled at her again, but this time there was more strength in her expression. "No, don't be sorry, sweetie. He saved you, and I'm glad you're okay. He always loved you, you know, ever since you were little kids. All these years, he wouldn't stop chattering away about you. He was so happy when you agreed to be his girlfriend. At least he had that in his final coherent moments. He had love and someone he was willing to risk his life for, and that's all I ever could have wanted for my son. I'm so proud of him."

Despite Spencer's betrayal, he had saved her in the end. He risked his life to make sure she and her sister were safe. And because of that, Rose knew she would forgive him for working for The Midnight Flower. It was because of Spencer that she had a second chance to make amends with Lily and mend her broken family.

Rose leaned her head on Fiona's shoulder. "I'm proud of him too."

Rose and Spencer had known each other since they were three. Spencer had to survive. She couldn't imagine her life without his presence in it—his sparkling hazel eyes, the way he always did what she wanted even if it was dangerous or silly, how competitive he was when they played video games, the nights when they would sit side by side and silently read comics. If he didn't make it, she would miss all of it.

Chapter 61: Rose

Rose stayed in the hospital waiting room with Fiona for the rest of the day until she remembered her mom wanted her home for dinner.

"Do you want to join my family for dinner?" she asked Fiona before she left.

"No, that's okay. Go enjoy your time with your family," Fiona told her. "I'll stay here in case the situation changes."

"Will you let me know if—"

Fiona nodded before she finished the sentence, anticipating what Rose was about to ask.

"Thank you."

When Rose arrived at home, she ate dinner with her parents and sister. The evening was uneventful. After dinner, Lily went back into her bedroom after not uttering a single word during the meal. Rose contemplated checking on her, but decided against it. Her sister needed to wallow and come to terms with her new reality—one where she was a kidnapping victim, but also a survivor.

As Rose helped her mom clean up the kitchen and wash the dishes, her phone rang.

"Hello?" she said, answering the call after she saw it was from Fiona.

"Rose, he's out of surgery. The doctor said he's stable. Spencer will have a long road to recovery, but they expect him to pull through."

"Oh my God. That's great news! Thank you for letting me know," Rose replied. "Let me know if there's anything I can do."

Rose hung up. She squeezed her phone tightly and shoved it into her back jean pocket, then stormed up the stairs to her sister's room. There was something she needed to deal with.

Rose pounded her fists on the door until a bewildered Lily opened the door, pulling earbuds out of her ears.

"Yeah?" Lily said, not opening the door all the way.

Rose shoved past Lily and into the room. She turned to face her sister and pointed a finger at her accusingly. "Spencer almost died."

"He-he's . . . not going to make it?" Lily asked, apparently shocked, because her voice shook as she closed the door.

"No, but he got lucky! He lost a lung and part of his heart, so what do you think that means? Are you listening to me? Did you know Spencer was working for him? Did you know what falling in love with him and then losing him would do to me? Did you think about that? Or did you not think any of this through and just went along with whatever Mr. Mortensen told you to do?" Rose raged, pacing Lily's bedroom.

Lily sat on the edge of her bed, staring at her timidly, not speaking.

"You were tricked and manipulated and conned in every way, Lily. Mr. Mortensen didn't love you. He didn't think you were special. He tried to do the same to me, and to who knows how many other girls. The police are still searching his house, but they called earlier asking me if I knew about his secret room. They found an entire room full of photos and mementos from other young girls, so they're searching the rest of the property now. He might have buried them at his house." Rose pointed a finger at her. "You weren't the only one. He went after you because you were easy. Because you fell for it, and he knew you wouldn't fight back."

Lily's lower lip trembled, and she finally replied. "You don't know what you're talking about, Rose. I think . . . I think I had to convince myself I loved him because if I didn't, then I was stuck there, not allowed to leave. I didn't get to go outside for a year. Do you know how much I missed out on? How many times I asked him to take me to the mall, a movie, anywhere outside of his house? If I misbehaved or argued with him, he locked me in the guest room. The only window in there was bolted shut. I tried to escape every chance I got, but I . . . I didn't make it very far. Do you know what my punishment was? He kept me locked in the bedroom for two days without food."

Rose faltered in her misplaced anger. "Lily, I—"

"You don't know what it was like in there, Rose, and I hope you never have to go through something so traumatic. I'm sorry about Spencer. Whenever James had people over, he didn't let me out of the bedroom, so I didn't know what went on. I knew people were working for him, or doing favors for him. I heard Spencer's voice one time, but I was locked in the spare bedroom, so what was I supposed to do? It should be a small comfort to you that in the end, Spencer chose you. In the end, Spencer took the bullet meant for you, so you could live."

A sob wrenched its way out of Rose's throat.

"So do that! Live! Don't let Spencer's betrayal or James's schemes, or Holly, Reggie, Kylar, Mason—any of them—get to you. Move on from the past. Blame me if you want to, but I'm trying to deal with this too," Lily said, lifting her chin defiantly and glaring at her.

Rose lurched forward, enveloping Lily in a hug. Lily hugged her back, gently at first, but soon, her arms wrapped around Rose in a tight embrace. The two sisters stood there, clinging to each other and sobbing for what seemed like hours to Rose.

Eventually, they broke apart, and Rose sat down on Lily's bed. Her gaze drifted around the room. Her mom must have cleaned in there recently because the surfaces weren't dusty, and the carpet had fresh tracks on it as if it had been recently vacuumed.

Lily peeked through the purple, lacy curtains covering one of her bedroom windows. "The sun is setting," she said softly. "Tomorrow is a new day." She remained at the window, her hand holding the curtain back so she could watch the sun set.

Rose followed her sister's gaze out the window. Pink, red, and orange hues sank down the skyline, until the darkness crept in, covering the beauty of the day for the night to take over.

Rose didn't know how any of them would move on from this. She didn't know how to move forward. She didn't know if her sister would ever be a fully functioning person who could let go of thinking she had found love—love that had turned out to be a lie. Similarly, Rose's love had also turned out to be a lie, in the way that mattered, at least. If Spencer had been honest with her or not agreed to work for Mr. Mortensen, not agreed to give up her secrets, how differently would this all have turned out?

If Spencer survived, how could she trust him again?

Lily's hand dropped from the curtain, and she faced Rose with a small smile playing across her face. The first genuine smile she had seen from her sister in quite some time. "We'll move on, right? Together?"

"Together," Rose promised, not wanting to shatter the illusion, the promise of a new day to her little sister. She had failed her once, but she wouldn't make that mistake again. Rose would protect her. She would stand by Lily's side no matter what happened in the days to come.

Because in the end, the darkness always took over. Even if the villain was dead, his mark remained on them forever.

Note from the Author

Hi Reader! Thank you so much for reading my latest thriller book. If you want to help me, I would appreciate it immensely if you wrote an honest review for *Dead Girls Can't Smile*. Posting your review online is one of the best ways to support indie authors. Reviews help other readers decide which books they want to buy and allow indie authors to gain more exposure to new readers. Please consider posting a review on the book retailer website where you purchased the book and/or on Goodreads.

Acknowledgements

If you've read one of my books, you probably know who I want to thank first. I'm incredibly thankful for my wonderful, wonderful husband, Zed. I'll forever be grateful that he agreed quitting my full-time job was the right move, so I could write full-time. I know not everyone is as blessed as I am to have such a supportive partner, and I don't take that for granted. I couldn't do this without his unwavering support and love.

Rocking Book Covers designed the cover for *Dead Girls Can't Smile*. They have been great to work with for my past two books and have made the cover design process so easy.

Sarah, owner of Three Owls Editing, has now edited three of my books. I'm so happy I finally found an editor I can trust. She always catches my mistakes and cleans up my writing.

My amazing beta readers: Robert, Alexis, and Evelyn. Each of them has beta read multiple books I've published, and I couldn't be more thankful for their help. They always pinpoint exactly what is missing and help me strengthen my writing. I appreciate their willingness to read my crappy early drafts and for being honest with me about what needs to be changed.

And finally, to you, my readers. Whether you've been reading my books since *The Long Shadow on the Stage* was published in 2020 or this is the first Nichole Heydenburg book you picked up, I appreciate your support so much. I hope you were able to escape reality for a few hours and that you enjoyed the twists and turns.

Subscribe

If you're interested in being a part of the first group of readers to learn about:

- My upcoming book releases and works in progress

- Cover reveals and ARCs

- Exclusive book content

- Book sales and freebies

- Giveaways

- In-person book events

Sign up for my newsletter on **www.nicholeheydenburg.com**!

Made in the USA
Middletown, DE
03 July 2025

10082600R00177